The Devil Wears Stretch Pants

A Val Fremden Humorous Mystery, Volume 4

Margaret Lashley

Published by Zazzy Ideas, Inc., 2025.

Copyright

More Mysteries by Margaret Lashley

Available on Amazon in Your Choice of Ebook, Paperback, Hardback, or Audiobook.

Val Fremden Humorous Mysteries Spinoff Series (in order)

- That Time I Kinda Killed a Guy
- There's Something About Gary
- Show Me the Funny Money
- The Devil Wears Stretch Pants
- More to come!

https://www.amazon.com/dp/B0CG648N16

New to Val Fremden? Don't miss the series that started it all!

The Val Fremden Midlife Mysteries (Nine-Book Series)

https://www.amazon.com/gp/product/B07FK88WQ3

Doreen Diller Mystery Trilogy (Three-Book Series)

https://www.amazon.com/gp/product/B0B2X3G3G7

Freaky Florida Investigations (Eight-Book Series)

https://www.amazon.com/gp/product/B07RL4G8GZ

What Fans Are Saying About The Val Fremden Mystery Series

- *"A hilarious, mile-a-minute ride alongside well-drawn characters with great friendships and a bit of romance on the side. Margaret never fails to deliver!"*
- *"Thanks, Margaret, for this wonderful character. Sometimes I think she's me!"*
- *"The problems (Val) encounters are so weird, only her brain could go that route. She is paranoid, but honest. Weird but wonderful. Her friends are a real hoot. I don't know where she finds them, but I want some too. They are so much fun!"*
- *"Weird and quirky, that's Val. Wonderful read (for) anyone needing a good laugh and an adventure into the weird."*
- *"I have read many of the Val Fremden books, and whilst events in past books have led her to this point it is possible to read each book as a standalone. However, I urge you to read this fun series, Val is a totally unique character, fun, slightly mad and definitely old enough to behave better (but she doesn't!)."*
- *"Margaret's observations and witty turn of phrase make this book a laugh-a-minute."*

Prologue

They say you never know what you have until it's gone—or until you're forced to clean out your closets. While I was fishing around in mine today, I didn't find any skeletons, but I *did* find a few ghosts from my past ...

Namely, my Wrench of Wrath, my Plyers of Pain, and my Ice Pick of Insanity—each a contender in my lifelong endeavor to find a non-homicidal way to placate the rage brought on by, well, *being alive*.

Each of these earlier prototypes had been summarily retired when I'd discovered the deeply satisfying, soul-freeing deliciousness of smashing figurines to bits with my Hammer of Justice. And now I'd struck upon another brilliant idea.

I was about to *merchandise my madness*.

I was about to become the official co-owner and operator of a retail establishment where anyone off the street could rent a room full of junk by the half-hour and sling a hammer at it to their heart's content.

Come on. It's no crazier than collecting Beanie Babies. And it's a whole lot healthier than eating your weight in Snickers bars.

Besides, you know you want to.

Chapter One

I stood staring at a freckled butt-crack. It was peeking up above the waistband of a pair of droopy jeans. Momentarily mesmerized by morbid fascination, I almost got whacked in the kneecap by the back-end of a flailing hammer.

"Hey! Watch where you're swinging that thing!" I yelled at Winky.

My pudgy, ginger-haired friend was on his knees, driving a sizeable nail into a wooden beam. Winky was hard at work framing in the walls that would divide Belated Rooms thrift shop into two separate retail spaces.

The front half would remain under the management of my new business partner, Geraldine Jiggles. There, she'd continue to operate her dingy second-hand shop. But the back half, behind the new wall under construction, was where I'd be setting up my new "retail therapy" enterprise, *Simply Smashing*.

Winky gave the nail another *whack*, driving it deep into the wooden joist. Then, with a pig-like *grunt*, he rose to standing, hiked up his jeans, and said, "That's kinda ironical, don't you think?"

My left eyebrow flatlined. "What are you talking about?"

Winky grinned and held up his hammer. "You tellin' me to watch where I swing this thang. That's the whole point a this new place a yours, ain't it? To hit whatever you want with a hammer?"

I smirked. "That excludes *humans*." I bit my bottom lip and added, "Except maybe for Geraldine."

Winky chuckled. "Uh-oh. Trouble in paradise already?"

"Maybe."

I turned and shuffled away from the construction zone, past racks of smelly clothes and tables laden with the kind of useless junk that would make perfect fodder for my new smash shop.

As I reached the yellowed plexiglass checkout counter at the front of the store, I glanced down at a scrap of notebook paper lying on the counter beside the huge black cash register. Scribbled on it was the un-flattering doodle of an old woman wearing plastic croc shoes and devil horns. I'd been working on it all morning. I picked it up, studied it, and let out a sigh.

"What's wrong, Val-Pal?" Winky asked.

Lost in thought, I hadn't realized he'd been trailing behind me. I turned to face him. "Geraldine, that's what's wrong." I frowned. "Given that I'm helping save her thrift shop from bankruptcy, I thought she'd let up on her condescending attitude toward me."

Winky shrugged and smiled good-naturedly. "You can't expect an old dog to learn a new trick on the very first try."

"I know. But I was hoping she'd at least consult me before she dragged in any more garbage off the street."

Winky cocked his freckled face. "What'cha mean?"

I nodded toward the front door. "See that ugly wingback chair over there? Geraldine hauled it in here this morning without even consulting me." I scratched an itch on my elbow. "I think it has fleas. What if my customers get bitten?"

Winky grinned. "Well, you know that old saying."

"What? 'One man's trash is another man's treasure'?"

Winky shook his head. "Nope. 'If it's free, it's for me.'"

I laughed despite myself. Winky had a way of finding the light at the end of the tunnel, even if that light turned out to be the glow from of a pair of demon eyes.

I'd just signed a year's contract to share a workspace with my former boss, Geraldine Jiggles. The scrawny, seventy-something woman had been a tyrant to work for, but we were supposed to be equals now. Even so, I had a sinking feeling that if I wasn't careful, things between her and me could quickly devolve into a junk-strewn hellscape.

I took another glance at the butt-sprung, black-and-white-striped wingback chair, then laid my sketch of the she-devil face-down on the checkout counter. I took a deep breath and tried to adopt Winky's positive, can-do attitude.

"You're right, Winky. Geraldine simply saw an opportunity with that chair and took it. You know, with a few throw pillows and a shawl draped over it, that hideous thing just might be salvageable."

Winky grinned. "Now *that's* what I'm talkin' about! Hey, where'd you get such a weird idea, anyways?"

"To use throw pillows on the chair?"

"No. To charge people to beat the tar outta stuff."

"Oh." I smiled. "I got it from this woman named Tat. She came into the thrift shop last week looking for stuff to smash. She said the place she usually went to in Tampa was closed due to illness."

Winky smirked. "Lemme guess. Somebody got their teeth knocked out?"

I grimaced. "Uh ... I didn't think to ask. Anyway, Tat told me that smash rooms were the cheapest mental-health therapy she'd ever experienced."

"What other kind had she gotten?"

"Uh ... again, I didn't ask."

Winky shot me a conspiratorial wink. "I tell you what. If'n I cain't fix something I'm workin' on, I've been known to give it a good whack or three before I throw it in the dumpster. Kinda takes the edge off a failin'."

I grinned. "Exactly! And that's the kind of therapy I'm going to offer my customers!"

"You could be on to somethin' for sure," Winky said.

I glanced up at the half-built wall that would soon define the space for my very own shop. "Seriously, Winky. Meeting Tat was like meeting a kindred spirit. She was like an angel sent down from heaven to tell me, 'Val Fremden, *this* is what you were born to do.'"

Winky rubbed his chin thoughtfully. "Kinda like when Laverne met her blessed Lady of the Weiner Wagon, huh?"

(Don't ask.)

My upper lip hooked skyward. "Uh ... yeah. Actually, exactly like that."

Winky smiled and put a hand on my shoulder. "I get it, Val-Pal. I felt the same way when me and Winnie opened up our donut and fishin' bait shop. Some thangs is just natural-born meant to be."

Chapter Two

I shifted Shabby Maggie, my ragged, 1963½ Ford Falcon Sprint convertible, into reverse and edged out of the parking space in front of Belated Rooms. I was on my way to meet my best friend Milly Halbert-Pansky at her accounting firm of Griffiths & Maas. She and her husband Vance had agreed to loan me $5,000 to help start up my new venture, Simply Smashing.

As I slowly cruised past the quaint little shops lining Corey Avenue, a niggling fear made my gut begin to flop like a skydiver about to leap out of a plane with a torn parachute; I didn't want to disappoint Milly.

I haven't had a real job in years. Do I have what it takes to be a businesswoman anymore?

A block from my destination, I pulled up to a stop sign and took a noisy slurp from my giant coffee cup. Then I checked my face in the rearview mirror.

I gasped.

Brown coffee lines edged both sides of my mouth like some caffeine-crazed version of *The Joker*. My teeth were light blue, thanks to a hastily gobbled blueberry Pop-Tart. And, worse yet, a glob of blueberry filling had tumbled down the front of my white T-shirt, creating a purple skid mark from my collarbone to the tip of my left boob.

Good grief! Forget qualifying as a businesswoman. Do I even meet the basic criteria of being a grown-up?

I pulled into the parking lot of Milly's accounting firm feeling as incompetent as Lucille Ball at that chocolate factory. But at least I was on time for my meeting.

I scrounged around in the glovebox for a paper napkin and wiped the crazy, java-man moustache from my lips. Scrubbed clean, I applied fresh lipstick. Then I fished my brush out of my purse and ran it through my frizzy, windblown hair.

From the neck up I looked better. But what could I do about my shirt?

I leaned over the front seat and rifled around in the back of the car for something to cover the incriminating blueberry stain. I spotted a slightly crumpled, short-sleeved shirt I'd filched from a bargain bin at the thrift shop a couple of days ago. I grabbed it, got out of the car, and slipped it on. It was too tight to button, so I left the shirt open over my T-shirt and headed to Milly's office.

"May I help you?" a snobbish voice rang out as I opened the door.

I looked up from tugging the wrinkled shirt over the blueberry mark. A familiar face stared at me from the receptionist's desk. It belonged to none other than my old nemesis Shirley Saurwein, the sarcastic, bleach-blonde, gum-cracking reporter for the *Beach Gazette*.

"What are *you* doing here?" we said in unison.

"Why are your teeth blue," Saurwein asked. "Eat a Smurf for breakfast?"

"Ha ha. Why are you working here? Finally piss off the wrong politician?"

"No," Saurwein hissed. "You might not be aware of this, Fremden, but journalism jobs don't pay squat nowadays. I took this gig as a ... temporary assignment. To supplement my income."

My right eyebrow rose a notch. "You work for Tiffany's Temps?"

Saurwein's eyebrows arched with surprise. "Yes. How did you know that?"

I smirked. "Maybe I'm a better reporter than you."

"With blue teeth? In your dreams."

I ran my tongue over my teeth. "Fine. I used to work for Tiffany myself."

Saurwein looked me up and down and shook her head. "They'll take anybody, apparently."

I stared right back at her. "*Apparently*."

"Wait a minute," Saurwein said. "You're not here applying for the receptionist job, are you? If so, you're too late. It's been filled. *By me.* Besides, you don't stand a chance dressed like that, Fremden. You look like you just climbed out of a dumpster." She let out a caustic laugh. "At your age, I bet you don't even know how to use a computer!"

I straightened myself up to my full five feet, four inches. "I'll have you know I was already offered the job," I said huffily, not even having to lie about it. "But I decided to open my own business instead."

Saurwein smirked. "*Sure* you did."

"*Whatever,*" I said, barely stifling an eyeroll. "Look. I'm here to see Ms. Halbert-Pansky."

"In that outfit?" Saurwein didn't even bother to hide her smug amusement. "What's the matter? Laundromat eat your clothes?"

"Just buzz her," I said.

"Do you have an appointment?"

"I don't—"

"Hush!" Saurwein hissed, putting a finger to her bright red lips. She punched a key on the phone system panel. "Ms. Halbert-Pansky? There's someone here to see you. I'm not sure, but I think she's applying to be the new cleaning lady? Or perhaps she's just a penniless panhandler."

Saurwein clicked off the phone and smirked. "She says you can go on back. First door on the left."

"Thank you for your lack of professionalism, as always," I said, then smiled serenely and turned on my heels. There was no point ramping up a battle of wits I knew I'd already won. Saurwein would find out Milly and I were best friends soon enough.

"Wait," Saurwein said as I turned toward the hallway. "Is that a *bullet hole* in the back of your shirt?"

I froze in my tracks.

Well, maybe just one more cheap shot.

I turned around and smiled at Saurwein. "A bullet hole? And here I thought your back-stabbing weapon of choice was a knife."

. . . .

AFTER MY CATTY RUN-in with Shirley Saurwein, it was good to see Milly's friendly face. Unlike the has-been reporter, Milly wasn't so shallow as to judge someone on their appearance, even though she prided herself on her own. We were best friends. I didn't have to make a good first impression. I walked down the hall and tapped lightly on her office door.

"Come in!" she called out.

I stepped inside and smiled. "Hey, Milly."

Milly cocked her head slightly and appeared confused. "Val? I thought you were the new cleaning lady."

I grimaced. "That was just a joke."

"A joke? I don't understand. Why do you seem dressed for the job?"

My ears caught fire.

Crap on a cracker!

I'd shown up for a business loan wearing the kind of rags most people wash their car with! Why had I just thrown on the first clean thing I'd found in my closet? I closed my eyes with shame.

It's official. I'm not a businesswoman. I'm a moron!

"Um ... the cleaning lady thing was a bad joke," I backpedaled. "By your new receptionist, Shirley Saurwein."

Milly's face registered surprise. "You *know* her?"

"Yeah. From the *Beach Gazette*."

"What's that?"

"A little neighborhood newspaper. She's a part-time reporter for them. She's run a few articles about me in the paper. *Unflattering* articles, I might add."

"Oh." Milly's lips curled into a pensive frown. "Like what?"

I shrugged sheepishly. "Long story short, I used to work at Tiffany's Temps. I got a reputation there as The Closer. I thought it was for nailing interviews and landing jobs. But it turned out I was called The Closer because the businesses I worked for tended to close their doors for good shortly thereafter."

Milly's blonde eyebrows rose an inch. "Are you serious?"

"Um ...yeah. The owner, Tiffany Darnell? She called me, 'The retail version of the Grim Reaper.'" I grimaced. "I have a copy of the article if you want to see it."

Milly stared at me, aghast.

I took a step backward. "Uh ... if you don't want to loan me the money now, I understand."

"What?" Milly blinked like a stunned deer, then her eyes focused back on me. "No. I just ..."

"Don't believe everything you read, Milly," I pleaded. "Saurwein's got the personality of a wet mole rat. You think this outfit is bad? The woman once rode me like a pony while she was dressed in nothing but a T-shirt and a dirty diaper!"

"What?" Milly's face froze in horror.

Oh, crap! I think I finally broke her!

"Milly?" I said softly, leaning over her desk. "Please, forget everything I just said. It's not relevant to our situation."

"Huh?" she asked, her perfectly manicured fingers fidgeting with a button on her expensive tailored blouse.

"There's only one thing you need to know about Shirley Saurwein," I said.

Milly looked up at me. "What's that?"

"She just told me I was so old I probably didn't even know how to use a computer."

Milly looked perplexed. "So?"

"You and I are the same age, Milly."

"What?" she said. Then her eyes suddenly lit up. I nearly squealed with relief as I watched my best friend's fighting spirit reboot.

Milly gasped. "Why that little snit!"

I smirked. "Finally, you see her like I do."

Milly sighed. "What makes her so witchy?"

"I dunno. Maybe she was born with it. Maybe it's amphetamines."

We both laughed for a second, then I slapped on my most serious businesswoman face.

I sat down in the chair in front of Milly's desk. "I have to admit something to you. Maybe Saurwein's kind of right. Maybe I don't have what it takes to run a business anymore."

Milly smiled softly and took my hand. "I know you've got it in you, Val. You only have to believe in yourself."

"But I feel so ... unqualified."

"That's how I know you'll make it!" Milly shot me a motherly smile. "Someone once told me that when you're willing to do what you're un-qualified to do, *that's* what qualifies you."

My nose crinkled. "Sounds kind of counterintuitive to me. But I'm grateful you believe in me."

Milly grinned. "I do. I totally do."

I smiled. "Saurwein's wrong, by the way. I *do* know how to use a computer."

"Of course you do!" Milly glanced at the blueberry stain on my left boob. "Still, maybe you should consider getting a uniform."

"For Simply Smashing?"

"Yes. You know, to represent your brand. Maybe some cute overalls with a clean pink shirt underneath. And your hair pulled up in a bow, like *Rosie the Riveter* only pinker!"

"That's not a bad idea," I said, admiring Milly's crisp, elegant attire. "You always look so put together, Milly. And you make it look so ef-fortless."

She laughed. "That's because you don't see all the prep work that goes into it before I walk out the door in the morning."

My nose crinkled. "Prep work?"

"Of course. You don't think I just stumble out of bed and rummage through my closet looking for a clean shirt, do you?"

I grimaced. "Uh ... you don't?"

"Of course not! I plan each outfit down to the matching panties! And when I get to work, I take ten minutes to visualize how I see my day going."

"You do?"

"Absolutely!" Milly wagged a manicured finger at me. "That's how I achieve both the *look* and the *outlook* for success! Speaking of which, here's the paperwork to sign for your loan."

I smiled at her sheepishly. "I want to thank you and Vance again for this. I'm going to do my best to be a success."

"I'm glad to hear that. Because success doesn't come from luck or chance, Val. It comes from being prepared and ready to strike when an opportunity presents itself. You know, like the one you have now with Geraldine."

I looked up at her hopefully. "So you really believe in the business idea?"

Milly blanched. "If I didn't, I wouldn't be handing you five grand now, would I?"

"No, I guess not." I leaned across the desk and signed the paper she shoved my way.

"Good," Milly said, beaming at me. "I'll have Ms. Saurwein make copies. Val, I'm so proud of you. This is serious, grown-up stuff you're doing. But I have to warn you, half of all new business ventures fail within the first year. We need to make sure that doesn't happen to you."

I gulped. "How can we do that?"

"With this." Milly slid a small binder across the desk at me.

"What is it?"

"A plan, Val. I made you daily, weekly, and monthly routine sheets to follow."

Geez. I don't even have a solid plan for the rest of this afternoon ...

"Follow your daily plans and the weekly and monthly ones will take care of themselves," Milly said with more enthusiasm than I'd managed to muster about anything in my life.

I glanced inside the binder. The first page was a list of rules for success. The first one was:

1. *Arrive on time, and with a smile.*

"Here's a little tip," Milly said, sliding a pack of gum across her desk at me. "Blue teeth are a no-no. This stuff will take those stains right off."

I took the whitening gum and flipped through the binder. "I really appreciate this. It might take me a little while to figure it all out."

Milly nodded. "I understand. But here's the bottom line. Make $2,200 a month. That will cover your loan principal and interest, rent, utilities, insurance, and operating and advertising expenses."

I looked up from the dizzying array of charts in the binder. "What about my salary?"

Milly chuckled. "Simple. You want a salary? Make more than $2,200. Your salary will be whatever you have left over."

I gulped. "That sounds like a lot of work just to break even."

Milly smiled softly. "It might feel like it at first. And you're right. It will be a lot to juggle. And you'll have to give it your all to succeed. But here's a little secret; when you find your niche, working doesn't feel like work!" She glanced around her office, her eyes bright with delight. "You see, accounting doesn't feel like work to me."

I tried to contain my horror. "What does it feel like?"

"Victory, Val. Victory! You know what I mean?"

I grimaced. "I might if I'd ever actually *had* a victory."

Milly laughed. "Oh, come on now, Val. You used to be a high-roller advertising writer. That's a skill that should come in handy now. Neglecting to advertise is a huge reason many businesses fail."

"I know." I nodded, feeling my confidence growing. Advertising was familiar territory. "Not advertising is like throwing a party but forgetting to invite anyone. Nobody knows about it unless you tell them."

"See? You sound like a pro already." Milly wagged her eyebrows. "And I have to say, I've never seen anyone as good at wielding a hammer as you. You should be a *smashing* success."

I smiled. "Thanks for the pep talk, Milly."

"You're welcome. You're a businesswoman again, Val. Remember, it's like riding a bicycle."

"Once you learn it, you never forget how?"

"Well, that, and it's definitely something you don't want to do when you're drunk."

I laughed, then stood up to go. "Hey Milly, I meant to ask. Did you manage to get Geraldine's balloon mortgage restructured?"

"Yes. Belittled Rooms is no longer in danger of popping."

"*Belated* Rooms."

Milly smirked. "Oh. Right. But don't forget. Geraldine is counting on your rent to help her make her own payment. Like it or not, you two are a team now. If she goes under, so does the space for *Simply Smashing*. It's a sink or swim proposition for you both."

I gulped.

I only hope neither of us is wearing lead underwear.

"Here are the papers you asked for," Saurwein said, barging into Milly's office. She slapped the copies of my loan on Milly's desk, shot me a sneer, then stomped out of the room.

"Classy," I quipped.

"Don't worry about Saurwein," Milly said, picking up the loan papers. "As soon as you leave, I'm going to tell her it isn't working out. As your bestie, I've got your back, Val."

"Thanks." I took the copy of the loan Milly handed me. "With any luck, her and my paths will never cross again. But if I'm honest, Milly, I can be just as sarcastic as Saurwein."

"No," Milly said, shaking her head. "There's a difference."

My back straightened. "A difference?"

"Absolutely. You don't have true malice in your heart, Val. Sure, you might take a jab at someone now and then. But you'd never stab them in the back when they're down."

I smiled. "Thanks for believing in me—in more ways than one."

"You're welcome." Milly grabbed a tape measure from her desk drawer. "Now, stand still. I want to get your measurements. I'm going to order you some cute T-shirts and overalls on Amazon."

"Fine." I succumbed to Milly's charm and raised my arms out to my sides. "While you're at it, could you order me a couple of life rafts, too?"

Chapter Three

"Is he about done turning this place into a pig sty?" Geraldine grumbled as she came stomping through the front door of Belated Rooms. "Just look at all the dust and dirt everywhere!"

"All that grime was here before Winky ever got started," I said.

"And whose fault is *that*?" Geraldine shot me some side-eye as she shuffled by in her mismatched polyester clothes and neon-green Crocs. I'd swear, if plastic had never been invented the woman would probably have been walking around naked as we spoke.

I shook my head to clear away the mental image.

Cut it out, Val. Play nice. You're a professional businesswoman now!

I took a deep breath and vowed not to get sucked into Geraldine's vortex of crabbiness.

"Don't worry, Geraldine," I said. "I'll make sure everything is cleaned up when the construction's done."

The old woman scowled. "You'd better! I shouldn't even have to tell you that." She glowered at me. "Fremden, you might be running your own place now, but you're still supposed to take care of the thrift shop while I'm out. And part of that job is cleaning up around here!"

"I know," I said, trying my best not to sound defensive.

I wondered why in the world Geraldine was extra moody today. I'd have asked her, but I didn't want to have my head ripped off my neck. Instead, I pursed my lips and kept them sealed tight. This "all for one, one for all" stuff was going to be harder than I'd bargained for.

I watched with wary eyes as Geraldine slammed her old purse down on the plexiglass checkout counter. The impact resounded through the building like a gunshot blast.

"I'm going down the block to see Davy Eber," she said. "Think you can you keep your friend there from destroying the place until I get back?"

I glanced over at poor Winky. His flabbergasted face was as red as a baboon's bottom. "Yes, I can do that."

"Good." Geraldine aimed her beady laser eyes at Winky. "No offense, young man, but I don't like my daily routine being disturbed with all this nonsense."

"Yes, ma'am," Winky said. "I should be done by the end of the day."

"Finally, some good news," Geraldine said, throwing her hands up. Without another word, she stomped out the door.

"Lordy," Winky said as the door closed behind her. "Who put a bee in her bonnet?"

"Bee?" I said. "My money's on the whole hive living in there."

Winky grimaced. "Is she always that cranky?"

"No. Sometimes she's unconscious."

Winky laughed. "Hey, who's Davy Eber?"

"He owns the antiques store a few shops down. Eber Antiques?"

"Nope. Can't say I ever have."

"Huh?"

Winky picked up the piece of paper on which I'd doodled the image of Geraldine with horns and flipped it over. My heart lurched at the realization of how close Geraldine had come to seeing it.

Winky laughed at my silly drawing. "That Geraldine sure is an ornery old cuss. No wonder won't no man marry her. It'd be like gettin' hitched to a wagonful a sandspurs."

I sighed. "Tell me about it. And now I'm in business with her." I shook my head. "What was I thinking?"

Winky laid the doodle back on the checkout counter. "Why'd you start working for her in the first place?"

"Blackmail." I blew out a breath. "That, and she didn't require a background check."

Winky's left eyebrow shot up. "I guess that knife done cut both ways, didn't it?"

I studied Winky for a second. "What do you mean?"

"You didn't check *her* out either. What perzacktly do you know about that old lady, anyways?"

I frowned. "What are you getting at?"

"It may be Monday mornin' quarterbackin' on a Thursday afternoon, but it might behoove you to figure out what makes Geraldine tick. You know, so's you can avoid settin' off her timebombs."

I nearly blanched. "You make a pretty good point, Winky. Speaking of which, you and I'd both better get back to work before she comes back and detonates."

Winky saluted. "I'm on it, ma'am."

He turned to go, and I picked up Geraldine's purse to stow it under the checkout counter. To my surprise, the thing weighed at least ten pounds! Curious, I snuck a peek inside. From beneath a worn leather wallet and half a dozen tubes of lipstick, something silvery glinted in the fluorescent lighting.

"You snoopin' on Miss Geraldine?" Winky asked.

Startled from being caught red-handed, I looked up to see him standing belly-up to the counter.

"I thought you were getting back to work!" I grumbled.

Winky's thin lips curled into a sly grin. "I was. But then I seen you peekin' in Geraldine's purse and got me a touch of the nozies, too. What'd you find in there?"

I snapped the pocketbook closed. "Just the usual stuff. Hairbrush. Coupons for Geritol." I hefted the purse up by its strap. "I think she must have a couple rolls of quarters in the bottom of this thing."

"For parkin' meters?"

"More likely so she can bean people with her purse when she gets mad, just like my mom used to do."

Winky raised a ginger eyebrow.

I frowned. "What? It's perfectly normal!"

"If'n you say so. But when *my* momma got mad, she just burned the biscuits."

I smirked. "You can't ward off enemies with burned biscuits."

Winky waggled his eyebrows. "You can if'n you can throw 'em hard enough."

I laughed and shoved Geraldine's purse into a cupboard under the cash register. "Look, I wasn't snooping. I was just ... following your advice. I was trying to find out more about Geraldine so I can avoid pushing her buttons."

"Uh-huh." Winky eyed me with skepticism. "I don't know about you, but when I wanna get to know somebody better, I usually just *talk* to 'em."

I groaned. "I've *tried*, Winky. But when it comes to talking about her past, Geraldine is like trying to break into Fort Noxious."

Winky chuckled. "Hey, I got an idea. Why don't you take the old lady to lunch? Give her a compliment or two. Better yet, y'all go shopping together. See a movie or something. It'll give me time to finish off the renovations. And you two can get to know somethin' about each other besides what aggravates the stew outta both of you."

I grimaced. "I dunno."

"Come on," Winky said, hitching up his jeans. "What's the harm in that?"

I chewed my bottom lip. If I couldn't make it work with Geraldine, I'd fail, and never be able to pay Milly back. I didn't want to do that to my best friend!

"But what if it doesn't work?" I asked.

Winky grinned. "Then we can switch to Plan B."

"Plan B?"

"Yeah. We can do us a stakeout!"

Chapter Four

Trying to get on Geraldine's good side was like trying to find Bigfoot. Did it even *exist*?

I took a sip of iced tea and stared at the scrawny old woman across the table from me as she gnawed on a fried chicken leg like a skunk-haired Tasmanian devil. Would she chew *me* up next?

As I munched on my club sandwich, I began to wonder if I should just cut my losses now. I could give Milly back her check for $5,000 and nip this whole business-partnership disaster in the bud.

But then what would I do? Arm-wrestle Saurwein for that boring receptionist job at Milly's accounting firm? I'd learned from our prior throw-downs that the sassy reporter was stronger than she looked.

"What are you looking so horrified about?" Geraldine barked, sending my worry-plagued daydream skittering off like a cockroach ducking for cover under a fridge.

"Huh?" I grunted, wiping mustard from my mouth with a paper napkin. "What are you talking about?"

Geraldine sucked a piece of chicken free from between her front teeth. "You look like you just swallowed a chum bucket."

Without warning, hot tears filled my eyes. I blinked them back. "Geez, Geraldine. Why do you hate me so much?"

Geraldine blanched. "Hate you? I don't hate you!"

"Then why are you so cranky all the time?" I blotted my eyes with my napkin and sniffed. "Listen. If we're going to survive working together, something's got to change. I don't want to spend the rest of my life arguing with you. What is it about me that makes you so angry?"

Geraldine's face fell like a gut-punched soufflé. "Nothing. Geez. Don't take it personally, Fremden. I guess ... I guess I've just suffered through a lot of disappointments in my 72 years."

I sniffed. "Well, so have I."

"Yeah, but I've got a twenty-two-year head start on you." She blew out a breath. "Anyway, this isn't a competition."

"Not one *I* want to win, for sure." I blew my nose. "I don't mean to minimize your past, Geraldine. I've had my fair share of disappointments, too. And I don't need another colossal one like going bankrupt and losing my best friend's money! We have a good chance at succeeding at this together, but only if we can find a way to get on the same team."

Geraldine sighed, shook her head, and laughed bitterly. "I appreciate the optimism, kid. When you first told me about your idea, I thought we had a chance, too. But now that's shot to hell."

I blanched. "What? Why do you say that? We haven't even started yet!"

"You don't know about this, but I'd worked out a whole plan that was going to put us on the map." Geraldine looked down at the chicken bones on her plate. "But now it's as hopeless as this chicken coming back to life and crossing the road."

"Plan?" I sniffed. "What plan?"

Geraldine's face went flat, as if all the life in her had suddenly drained away. She sighed, then reached for her purse in the booth beside her. She dropped it on the table with a *thunk*.

"For the first time in my life, I'm out of ideas and out of hope," she said, digging around in her purse.

"What do you mean by that?" I asked. Suddenly, a horrific thought crossed my mind.

Oh my word! Does she have a gun in there? Is she going to end it all right in front of me? Or, worse yet, shoot me?

Stop it, Val. Stop imagining ridiculous things!

I smiled softly at Geraldine. "Look. I'm sure everything is going to work out."

But in an instant, I realized it may not.

Geraldine's trembling hand had just emerged from her purse and it was *indeed* holding a gun—and it was aimed right at me.

Chapter Five

S *weet baby jackalope! Geraldine's pointing a gun at me!*

"Don't do it!" I pleaded, backpedaling for all I was worth. "I'm sure we can work this out like reasonable adults."

"Huh?" Brandishing the snub-nosed revolver with a trembling hand, the scrawny old woman casually laid it on the table. "I was just gonna get out my wallet and spring for the lunch tab. But hey, if you want to pay that badly, knock yourself out."

"Wha???" I gasped, my heart in my throat.

"Now where are my breath mints?" Geraldine mumbled to herself. She looked down and began digging through her purse again. I could still feel my pulse in my eyeballs when she pulled out a box of Tic Tacs and asked, "You want one?"

"Uh ... no thanks."

Geraldine tossed a Tic-tac into her mouth. "You know, Fremden, you could be right. I *have* been a bit ornery lately. Could be my blood sugar's low. Hey. I may be cranky, but at least *I* can *commit* to something."

In disbelief I was still alive, my back suddenly arched with indignation. "Wait a minute. *I* can commit, too!"

"Ha! Says the woman who only came to work for me because I blackmailed her." Geraldine stuck an elbow on the table and wagged a finger at me. "And who only stays because she owes me more money than she earns after taking her temper out on my merchandise!"

Geez. She had me there ...

While I sputtered trying to put together a comeback worthy of diffusing Geraldine's hard-truth bomb, the old woman tugged a rolled-up piece of paper from her purse. Yellowed and tattered around the edges, it looked like an ancient scroll.

"So, you don't think I take our partnership seriously?" Geraldine asked.

I grimaced. "It isn't that. It's just—"

"Well, take a look at *this*." She shoved the scroll at me. "That ought to change your mind."

I glanced down. My nose involuntarily crinkled. The battered scroll lying on the table between us appeared to have barely survived the meltdown of some past civilization.

If this is Geraldine's last will and testament, it must've been written when paper was still made out of papyrus!

"What is this?" I asked.

"Unroll it and see for yourself."

Hesitantly, I did as she instructed. As I unfurled the paper, I realized it was only printed to *look* old—unless, that is, they had sushi food trucks back in the Roman days.

"It's a poster for this year's Queen of the Road Survivalist Fair," Geraldine said.

My mouth fell ajar. "*Survivalist* fair? At your *trailer park*?"

"Yes." Geraldine's eyes narrowed. "Have *you* ever tried riding out a hurricane in a tin can, missy?"

Fair point.

"Uh ... no. But what's that got to do with—"

"Anyway, it doesn't matter now," Geraldine said, cutting me off. She blew out a tired, defeated breath. "This year's fair is gonna be cancelled."

"Cancelled?" I studied an image on the scroll. It was a gaggle of serious-faced seniors in old-timey clothes playing BINGO for canned goods. "Uh ... I'm sorry, Geraldine. But I'm still not following you. How was this fair thingy supposed to put us on the map?"

"Look down at the bottom," she said. "The main event is the Shootout at the Poke Corral."

I forced an indulgent smile, but I couldn't stop my wary eyes from taking another gander at the dull, short-barreled revolver still lying on the table beside Geraldine's purse. Its barrel was pointed right at my chest.

"A shootout," I said. "How ... *quaint*. Um ... speaking of guns, would you mind putting *that one* away now?"

"Huh?" Geraldine glanced down at the gun as if she'd never seen it before. "Oh. Geez. When did I ... never mind." She absently tucked the handgun into her purse and looked up at me. "So, you ready to go?"

"In just a sec," I said. "Um ... do you mind telling me why you're packing heat?"

"It's for the shootout competition. I mean ... it *was*." She sighed. "I've been practicing with it."

My eyebrows met my hairline. "You were practicing for a *shootout*?"

"Why wouldn't I?" Geraldine straightened her shoulders, then stabbed a thumb at her scrawny chest. "I could be a serious contender. I'll have you know you're looking at the sharp-shooter champion of the 1973 Vegas Vendetta games."

How I managed to keep my jaw from hitting the table, I'll never know. "Um ... okay. Fine," I said. "Whatever floats your boat, Geraldine. But I still don't understand—"

"The winner of the shooting competition gets a thousand bucks and their picture in the *Beach Gazette*," Geraldine explained. "I'm telling you, you can't *buy* that kind of publicity."

"Oh."

Geraldine frowned, sat back in the booth, and twiddled a chicken bone on her plate. "I thought we could use the winnings to promote both of our shops. But like I said, the whole fair's gonna be cancelled. My grand idea is as dead as these chicken wings."

I took another glance at the scroll and the image of the Poke Bowl food truck. "Why is it going to be cancelled?"

Geraldine's face puckered. "Orville Ledbetter, that's why."

I glanced up. "Who?"

"Orville Ledbetter. He's been the main sponsor of the fair for the last three years. But yesterday, he pulled out at the last minute." Geraldine shook her head. "Now the fair committee needs to come up with $4,500 by 5 p.m. today or the whole thing's dead in the water. Nobody I know has that kind of cash."

I raised a provocative eyebrow. "Are you *sure* about that?"

Geraldine studied me like a predatory insect. "What do you mean?"

I reached into my purse and pulled out the check for $5,000 I'd just gotten from Milly. I held it up for Geraldine to see. "You know what? Working together, I think we can keep this fair of yours on track."

Geraldine nearly spit out her dentures. "Are you for real?"

I winked. "Better than that. I'm *committed*."

"Nothing says committed like a big, fat check," Geraldine said, her beady gaze never leaving the check.

I could almost see the dollar signs dancing in her eyes.

Then Geraldine's thin, liver-spotted lips began to curl into a smile that scared me even more than the fact that she was packing a gun.

Chapter Six

After stopping by the bank to deposit Milly's check, it was all smiles and high-fives for me and Geraldine as we cruised back to Belated Rooms in Shabby Maggie like a scene right out of *Thelma and Louise*, minus driving off a cliff. (At least for now, anyway.)

"A good partnership is all about trust," Geraldine said, patting me on the shoulder, the sun glinting off her huge, pink sunglasses.

"It sure is!" I smiled at myself in the rearview mirror, then groaned. "Geez, Geraldine. Why didn't you tell me I had mustard on my nose before I went into the bank? You just said we could trust each other."

Geraldine shrugged. "Hey. I'm a junk dealer, not a makeup artist. For all I know, it could've been some new fashion trend."

"Argh!" I'd have argued the point if it weren't for the fact that the teller at the bank had been sporting a smiley face tattoo on her forehead. Geraldine was right. It appeared that nowadays, anything goes.

I cruised down Corey Avenue and found a parking spot a few spaces down from the dingy thrift shop we both now shared. Before I could even shift the convertible into park Geraldine sprang out of the passenger seat like a gray gazelle in stretch pants.

"I'll let the fair committee know it's back on!" she exclaimed, her gravelly voice a few octaves higher than normal. Grinning, she made a beeline for Belated Rooms, her lime-green Crocs slapping out a dull gallop on the hot asphalt.

"Great!" I yelled back, yanking the keys from the ignition. I shimmied out of the old Ford, then sprinted to catch up with Geraldine as she hoofed it to the front door.

"You get the show back on the road," I said, "and I'll take care of all the advertising and promotion!"

Geraldine whirled around. Her left eyebrow flatlined. "Wait a minute. You're supposed to be doing that already. Remember?"

Oh, I remembered all right.

In a classic Geraldine move, a few weeks ago the old woman had taken pictures of me and Shirley Saurwein during our dirty-diaper brawl to the death. Then she'd blackmailed us both by threatening to leak the photos to the media if we didn't do her bidding.

To save face, Saurwein had promised to give Geraldine free advertising space in the *Beach Gazette*. As for me, I'd saved my *own* hide by agreeing to write ads and articles promoting Belated Rooms—free of charge, of course.

Fast-forward to this exact moment, and I'd yet to write a single word singing the praises of Geraldine's run-down thrift shop. I'd been waiting for inspiration to strike me (or a meteor ... whichever came first). Anyway, now that I had $4,500 worth of skin in the game, I'd found my true inspiration—in more ways than one.

"Of course I remember," I said, forcing a smile. "What I *meant* was I'd start working on ad ideas for the *fair*, too. In fact, I should have a couple of concepts to share with you tomorrow. Does that work for you?"

"Not good enough," Geraldine growled. "The fair starts in two days. I want those ideas *today*."

She shoved open the shop's front door and shuffled over to the plexiglass checkout counter. After plunking her ugly vinyl purse down on it, she turned to face me again.

"All right, Fremden. First order of business. While I call the fair committee to tell them the good news, you need to call Saurwein and make nicey-nice with her."

Oh, holy crap-doodles. Not Saurwein!

"Why?" I whined.

"Because that woman owes us *free ad space*, that's why. Grab us a big slot in the Saturday edition. If she gives you any flack, remind her that if she doesn't want her dirty diapers aired in public, it's time to pay the piper."

"But I didn't lay no pipes," a man's voice rang out.

I turned to see Winky emerging from behind the newly construct-ed wall that now bisected Belated Rooms into two separate retail spaces. My pudgy, freckled friend scratched his head. "Did I miss some-thin'? Was plumbin' part of the project?"

"No," I said. "Geraldine was just using a figure of speech."

Winky nodded. "Oh. Well, then, I guess I should say, 'It's all over but the cryin.'"

My nose crinkled. "Are you hurt?"

"Nope. I'm done." Winky grinned. "That's a figure of speech, too, Val-Pal. At least in *my* circles it is." Winky nodded toward the new con-struction. "So, what do you gals think?"

I glanced past Winky. My eyes *boinged* open like a cartoon charac-ter's. "Wow! That's amazing!"

I'd been so busy dodging Geraldine's advertising bullets that I hadn't noticed what had been staring me right in the face. Winky had completed all the drywall work, and had even painted the new walls mint green, just like I'd asked.

Topping it off, above my new shop door hung the banner I'd had made at a print shop. Against a royal-blue background, white letters spelled out:

Simply Smashing ... Retail Therapy at Its Loudest!

"Oh, my goodness!" I gushed, and ran over to Winky. I took him by the forearms and we both jumped around for joy. "It's beautiful, Winky! I love it!"

"Not bad for amateur work." Geraldine's voice sounded from be-hind us, ending our little dance party like a needle scratching through a vinyl record.

Winky and I turned to face her. The skunk-haired mercenary pushed her neon-pink bifocals up on her nose, then unfurled her faux-ancient scroll atop the checkout counter like it was a treasure map.

"Geraldine!" I scolded. "Be nice to Winky. He did a great job."

"Hey, what you got there, Miss Geraldine?" Winky asked cheerfully, apparently not a bit bothered by her dig.

I pursed my lips. "It's a poster for a fair."

"The *Queen of the Road Survivalist* Fair," Geraldine said.

"No kiddin'!" Winky shuffled over to the checkout counter. "I been wantin' to go see me that shootout at the Okay Corral."

"The *Poke* Corral," Geraldine corrected. "It's sponsored by the Poke Bowl food truck."

"Speaking of sponsors," I said, sidling up to Winky and playfully elbowing him in the ribs. "Geraldine and I are the fair's main sponsors this year."

"You don't say!" Winky wagged his ginger eyebrows. "Think y'all can get me some free tickets?"

"Could be tough, seeing as there's no admission fee," Geraldine said, picking up the poster. "But help me tape this thing up on the front window and I'll see what I can do."

"All right!" Winky grinned, rubbed his hands together, then followed Geraldine toward the front of the shop.

I watched as Winky patiently held the fair poster in place against the glass while Geraldine, standing atop the seat of that old wingback chair she'd hauled in from gawd knows where, awkwardly taped the scroll's corners down. Together, they made quick work of the task at hand.

"Thanks," Geraldine said begrudgingly to Winky as she taped the last corner into place.

"Yes, ma'am," he said, beaming at the poster as Geraldine slipped the tape dispenser into her side pocket like a pistol into a holster.

Winky helped her climb down off the hideous wingback chair. Feet safely back on solid linoleum, Geraldine turned and patted one of the chair's dirty wings. "So, how do you like my latest acquisition?"

Winky studied the chair's black-and-white striped upholstery and said, "Kinda makes me hungry."

Geraldine eyed him like he was nuts. "*Hungry?*"

He nodded. "Yeah. Reminds me of the Hamburglar."

Geraldine grunted as if in pain. Then she rolled her eyes and marched over to the checkout counter. She snatched up her purse and said, "I'm outta here, you two knuckleheads."

"Where you goin'?" Winky asked.

Geraldine's nose rose an inch. "Not that it's any of your business, but as head honcho of the survivalist fair, I've got a lot of cold irons to get fired back up again."

"Ooo, I didn't know there was an ironin' competition!" Winky said. "Anything I can do to help out?"

Geraldine studied him for a moment, a dubious look on her face. "I don't know yet." She turned and glared at me. "As for *you*, Fremden, try to keep this place together while I'm gone. Get busy on those ads. And call Saurwein. *Do it now!*"

"Okay, already!" I grumbled.

Like chastised grunts drafted into Jiggles' army, Winky and I watched attentively as Drill Sergeant Geraldine stomped out the front door.

As soon as it creaked to a close, Winky shook his head and let out a long, low whistle. "For bein' equal partners, you sure do seem to be the one taking all the orders, Val-Pal."

I sighed. "Tell me about it." I flopped into the butt-sprung Hamburglar chair.

Winky laughed.

I frowned. "What's so funny?"

"With all them stripes, you look like you're in jail."

I folded my arms across my chest. "Kinda feels like it, too."

Winky grimaced. "I gotta say, that old woman's moods switch out faster'n tires in a NASCAR pit."

"Tell me something I *don't* know."

Winky rubbed his chin. "Well, now, did you know chickens are the closest livin' relatives to the T-Rex?"

"Huh?"

"You told me to tell you something you don't know. Did you know it?"

"No." I sighed. "All *I* know is that I've just committed to a year of running my new store inside Geraldine's thrift shop." I shook my head. "What have I done?"

"What'cha mean?"

"Honestly, Winky? I think *Geraldine* might be T-Rex's *second* closest living relative."

Winky laughed. "Could be. But I bet it's just a case of the Nervous Nellies. Poor old lady's got a lot a beans on her plate, what with runnin' this place and puttin' on that ironin' show and the fair and all."

"I guess you're right. It's probably just nerves."

Winky stuck a pudgy index finger into a hole in the Hamburglar chair's fabric. "Hey. Is that a bullet hole?"

I didn't even bother to look. "At this point, Winky, *nothing* would surprise me."

He laughed. "So, how'd you and Geraldine get so lucky as to sponsor the fair anyways?"

I scooted to the edge of the chair. "The original sponsor pulled out. Orville Ledbetter."

Winky's head cocked like a curious puppy. "That popcorn dude?"

"More like corn *hole* guy. He ditched the fair at the last minute. We stepped in to save it, but it cost me nearly all the money I borrowed from Milly to get Simply Smashing off the ground."

"I see. Then I guess you won't be liking this." Winky started to tuck a slip of paper into his shirt pocket. I snatched it away from him.

"What is it?" I asked.

He bit his bottom lip. "The bill."

"Three hundred and forty-seven dollars?" I asked, reading the sum aloud.

"That's just the cost of building materials. Sorry, Val-Pal. The price of stuff is sky-high these days. But like I told ya, my labor is on the house."

I frowned. "I can't let you do that, Winky."

"Course you can." He shrugged. "T'weren't nothin'."

"Yes it *was*! At least let me ... let me make dinner for you and Winnie."

Winky smirked. "How's about you *don't*, and we'll call it even."

I'd have argued that my cooking wasn't *that* bad, but even *I* couldn't swallow *that* whopper. I sighed and gave him a hug.

"Thank you, Winky. That leaves me with exactly $153 to start up my business. How am I gonna stock my whole shop with *this* measly sum?"

"No problem." Winky grinned and tapped a finger to his noggin. "You just gotta get creative, that's all."

My nose crinkled. "Creative?"

"Yep. Come with me. It's time we got busy junkerneckin'."

My nose crinkled. "Junkernecking? What's that? Redneck slang for making out in a landfill?"

Winky laughed. "Nope. We call *that* dump-humpin'."

I shook my head. "Sorry I asked."

Chapter Seven

I piled into Winky's battered blue van feeling like a naughty teenager playing hooky. No matter what lamebrained plan my redneck friend had in mind to help me stock my new shop, it *still* had to be a million times better than following Geraldine's orders to make nice with Shirley Saurwein.

"Just tell me one thing," I said as I slammed the passenger door with a *clunk*. "Is this juggernauting scheme of yours legal?"

Winky laughed. "*Junkerneckin*', Val-Pal. And sure it's legal. It's just like rubberneckin' at a fender-bender, 'cept we're gettin' us a good look at junk we spot lying on the side of the road. And it ain't by no accident. We're doing it *on purpose*."

"I see. Lovely." As I buckled my seatbelt, I spotted a proverbial fly doing the backstroke in the proverbial ointment. "But Winky, trash pickup is on Tuesdays and Fridays. Today is Thursday."

Winky grinned at me. "In *your* neck of the woods, maybe. But *every* day is trash day *somewheres*."

"Oh." I hadn't thought of that.

"Now, enough talkin'," Winky said. "Let's hit it."

He cranked the engine. The van coughed and shuddered to life. But as Winky reached for the gear shift, he froze. "Hey, ain't that Geraldine leaving that Eber guy's antiques store?"

I turned and peered through the grimy passenger window. Sure enough, a skunk-haired old woman emerged from Eber's Antiques an started bobbing down the sidewalk.

"You're right," I said. "I thought she was in a rush to meet up with the fair committee."

"Hmm." Winky rubbed his freckled chin. "Maybe she stopped by to sweet talk that old geezer into puttin' up one of those posters of hers in his window."

The image of Geraldine sweet-talking *anyone* nearly curdled my lunch. "Yeah, maybe. Hey, Winky. Do you mind if we hold off on the junkernecking for right now and check out what she's really up to?"

Winky's ginger eyebrows undulated like a pair of dancing caterpillars. "You mean spy on her? Like we was on a stakeout?"

I sighed. "Yeah, Winky. Like a stakeout."

"Hoo boy!" Winky hollered. "This day just keeps gettin' better and better!"

I couldn't agree more. All that's missing now is an extinction-level event.

• • • •

LIKE TWO LOW-RENT REJECTS from a cheap detective novel, Winky and I sat hunched and silent in his ratty blue van, keeping an eye on Geraldine as she bounced along the sidewalk, stopping in at every little shop along our little patch of Corey Avenue.

Given her outrageous tropical-print shirt, striped pants, and neon-green Crocs, Geraldine wasn't hard to spot amid the crowd of shoppers. But what the wily old skinflint was *up to* wasn't nearly as easy to make out.

After clomping her way up, then back down the block, Geraldine didn't head back to Belated Rooms. Instead, she climbed into her junky red pickup truck and took off in a cloud of rust-colored smoke.

"Oh, boy! There she goes!" Winky hollered. "Should we tail her?"

"Yeah, let's see where she goes. Maybe we can kill two birds with one stone."

"What 'cha mean?" Winky asked, turning the key in the ignition.

"We're after stuff for my shop, too. And it's been my experience that Geraldine can sniff out junk—"

"Like the Hamburglar can sniff out hamburgers?" Winky asked.

I nodded. "Yeah, Winky. Just like that."

• • • •

MAINTAINING A LOW PROFILE in a van the size of a juvenile blue whale wasn't easy. I nearly got seasick as Winky bobbed and weaved in traffic, following the trail of smoke that spewed from the tailpipe of Geraldine's old pickup.

Her first stop was at an ugly strip center on 49th Avenue. We pulled into the parking lot of the shop next door and hid behind an even dumpier van. From this vantage point, we watched as Geraldine made a quick dash inside a sketchy-looking beauty parlor called Curl Up & Dye.

"I don't get it," Winky said. "Is she gettin' her a haircut or makin' funeral plans?"

"Who says it can't be both?" I quipped, then gasped when Geraldine unexpectedly emerged from the beauty shop. "Quick! Duck!"

Peeking up over the bottom rim of the van's windows, we watched Geraldine get back into her truck. She sped out of the lot. We followed the belching pickup a few miles down 62nd Avenue until it made a sharp right onto Haines Road. About a half a mile down, Geraldine pulled into the Queen of the Road Trailer Park.

"Hey! I remember this place from our last stakeout," Winky said. "Don't Geraldine live here?"

"Yeah. She's probably meeting up with some of her fair cronies. Either that, or she's fixing to take a nap."

"Jackpot!" Winky yelled.

My nose crinkled. "You think she's taking a nap?"

"No!" Winky glanced around excitedly. "Lordy, look at all this free loot, Val-Pal. Turns out it's trash day in the trailerhood!"

I glanced past Winky to the left side of the road. It was littered with a hodge-podge of dead mattresses, busted furniture, and murderized kitchen appliances that had been mercilessly dragged out to the curb. Oddly, some had weeds growing up around them.

I nudged Winky. "I've got a feeling *every* day may be trash day here."

"Don't matter either way," Winky said. "We done hit us the junker-neckin' motherlode!"

Winky mashed the brakes and pulled the van to the side of the road beside a pile of junk the size of a cruise ship hot tub. Eyes bright with excitement, Winky hopped out, rubbed his hands together, and exclaimed, "All right! Let's do this thang!"

I glanced around to make sure Geraldine's truck was nowhere in sight, then reluctantly climbed out of the van and joined Winky. He was digging through the pile of household debris like a hog after truffles.

"Hey, you two! Keep your mitts off that stuff!" a man's angry voice rang out.

I looked up from examining a microwave oven that appeared to have been used to contain the detonation of a small nuclear device. From around the corner of the trailer in front of us, a guy came whizzing up on an orange riding mower.

"I've got an arrangement with the management," he said as he came rolling up. He tipped up the brim of his dirty straw hat to get a better look at us. "I get first pick around here."

Winky eyed the guy curiously. "No offense," he said, "but last time I looked, this was a free-junk country."

To my surprise, the mower guy's hard expression melted away with a shrug. "Eh, I guess it doesn't matter. I've already gone through today's stuff. You two knock yourselves out."

I glanced down at the heap of mangled household detritus and frowned. It was obvious that if there'd ever been anything worth swinging a hammer at in this pile, somebody else had already beaten me to it. My heart sank. I needed junk, and quick. I had my first client tomorrow morning at noon!

"Hey!" I called out to the man. "Who's your 'arrangement' with?"

"That's confidential," he said, then sucked on the gold front tooth gleaming from between his weathered lips. "But I'll tell you this much. I get paid ten bucks a box for sellable scrap."

The guy lifted one of his leathery hands from the mower's steering wheel and pointed a brown sausage-like finger toward the metal-mesh utility trailer he used to haul his lawn service equipment. About half of it was stacked with cardboard boxes full of junk.

I spotted an old vacuum-tube TV poking out of one of the boxes. My hammer hand began to twitch.

"What if I paid you more?" I blurted.

Mower guy took off his straw hat, revealing an enviable headful of slicked-back black hair. He shot me a gold-toothed smile and said, "Carl Menendez, at your service."

Chapter Eight

"Nice doing business with you, Carl," I said as we loaded the last box of junk into Winky's van. I handed the scrap man sixty bucks. "If all goes according to plan, I'll be needing more stuff every week."

Carl grinned and handed me his business card. "In that case, you can call me Rooster. Everybody around here does."

I smiled and shook his weather-worn hand. "Okay, Rooster. Tell me. How often do you collect stuff like this?"

Rooster folded the cash and stuffed it into a sweat-stained leather wallet. "Every day but my mowing days." He shoved the wallet into the back pocket of his jeans and climbed aboard his riding mower. "I usually collect junk here on Mondays and Thursdays and mow it on Fridays."

I cocked my head. "But today's Thursday. Why are you mowing *today*?"

"There's a big fair happening here this weekend," he said, adjusting his straw hat. "Starts up Saturday morning. The powers that be around here want everything ship-shape before then."

"Oh." I nodded. "Makes sense."

Rooster reached for the ignition on the mower.

"Wait!" I called out. "One more thing. Do you perchance *deliver*?"

Rooster glanced at the junk still left in his pull-behind equipment trailer. "Sure, why not? That is, if it's within a five-mile radius. Tell you what, if you buy $80 bucks worth, I'll deliver it for free. Otherwise, I'll have to charge you ten bucks extra for gas."

I smiled. "Deal. I'm opening up a new shop on Corey Avenue. I'll text you the address." I reached out and shook Rooster's strong, calloused hand again. "Sounds like the beginning of a beautiful relationship."

Rooster lowered his sunglasses and looked me up and down. "Could be." He winked, then pushed his glasses back up and cranked the ignition.

I looked over at Winky. He was staring at me, his eyebrows an inch higher than normal.

"What?" I asked.

Winky opened his mouth to say something, but Rooster beat him to it.

"Uh-oh," Rooster said, shifting gears on the mower. He was staring over my shoulder toward the road. "I better get a move on."

"Why?" I asked.

Rooster shoved the handle on the gear shift. "Sylvia don't like competition."

"What do you mean?" I asked, turning to look behind me.

An old woman on a bicycle was racing up the road toward us. The silver bun atop her head bobbed up and down as she pedaled furiously, her knobby knees nearly slamming into the straw basket attached to the front of the handlebars.

I whipped back around to face Rooster. "Is she the one you have the arrangement with?"

But Rooster couldn't hear me. He'd already taken off on his mower, hightailing it back behind the same trailer he'd appeared from earlier.

"What do you think that was about?" I asked Winky.

Winky eyed the woman barreling down the road toward us and slammed the back door of the van shut. "I ain't no expert on women," he said, scurrying toward the driver's door. "But I sure know me a mad hen when I see one."

I sprinted after him. "Mad hen?"

"Yep." Winky clamored into the driver's seat. "That there's a woman on the warpath."

I clambered into the passenger seat. "On the warpath with who?"

Winky shook his head and cranked the ignition. "I don't got no idea. But if'n it's *us*, I'm thinkin' it might behoove us to make like a pair of bananas and *split*."

I glanced in the side mirror at the woman on the bicycle. She was closer now. I could see her face was the color of a ripe pomegranate. She was waving her fist in the air, yelling something I couldn't decipher.

"Geez, Winky. I think you're right. Let's get the H E double tooth-picks outta here."

"I'm on it!" Winky punched the gas. We barreled down the main drag snaking through Queen of the Road Trailer Park, the raging, bun-haired bicyclist hot on our heels.

"We gotta lose her!" Winky said as we rounded a curve.

"No kidding." I grabbed onto the armrest to keep from flying out the open window. "Turn right here! *Now*!"

Winky hung a hairpin right. The van skittered onto a narrow side road. His teeth gritted with panic, Winky pulled into the first driveway we came to and slammed on the brakes beside a row of huge hibiscus bushes.

"Good lawdy," he whispered, cutting the ignition. "I hope we're hid good enough."

Winky's panic was contagious. I found myself wondering just how sour a pickle we were in. Had we broken some law? Had we run over that old lady's rose bushes or something?

Like a pair of sitting ducks, the two of us crossed our fingers, held our breath, and waited for Miss Hell on Wheels to pass by. After a minute or two of exchanging grimaces and wide-eyed glances, we suddenly heard the squeak of rusty bike pedals.

They were getting louder and louder.

"Oh no," I whispered. "I think she's heading right for us!"

"Hunker down," Winky whimpered as he slumped into his seat.

I followed his lead, keeping my eyes glued to the side mirror. I gasped. The same silver-haired woman suddenly appeared on the road at the end of the driveway. She stopped, blocking our escape with her bicycle.

"Oh, crap! What do we do now?" I squealed.

But before Winky could answer me, the old woman waved at us, then resumed pedaling down the road.

"Lord a mercy," Winky said, shaking his head. "If she'd a come for us, I don't know what I'd a done."

I cringed. "Me either!"

The danger over, the whole incident suddenly seemed totally absurd. I laughed out loud.

"Good grief, Winky, why were we so afraid of a little old lady on a bicycle?"

Winky cocked his head and stared at me. "Are you kiddin'? Come on, Val-Pal. Ain't you never seen *The Wizard of Oz*?"

I frowned. "Yeah. But that witchy woman on a bike wasn't *real*."

Winky shot me a knowing look. "Everything's real when you're a kid. You said it yourself. You was scared, too."

I frowned. "Okay, I *was* a little bit scared."

Darned old early childhood trauma. It's the worst!

Winky stuck his head out of the van window. "Looks like she's gone. Let's roll."

"Okay." As I reached for the seatbelt, I glanced around the sad little trailer park and felt grateful for my own tiny house made of concrete block. At least it stood a better chance of not going airborne in a tornado.

"You know, Winky. There was *one* thing that was for real in that movie."

Winky's eyes grew as big as boiled eggs. "Them flying monkeys? I *knew* it!"

"No! That old saying. There's no place like home."

Winky smiled and nodded. "I heard that."

Chapter Nine

After our ridiculous, narrow escape from our own idiocy, I told Winky it was time to ditch Queen of the Road Trailer Park and get back to work. We needed to unload the junk we'd scored from Rooster and I needed to get my new shop set up for my first client coming at noon tomorrow.

As we cruised down the trailer park's main street past mobile homes in various stages of upkeep and decay, I thought about scary Sylvia, the angry woman with the bobbing silver bun who'd scared the bejeebers out of us like the Wicked Witch of the West.

"Thank goodness that old woman wasn't after *us*," I said. "Still, I wonder what she was so darn mad about."

Winky chuckled. "I got me a theory."

"You do?"

"Yep. Ever hear that figure of speech, 'The only rooster in the hen-house?'"

"Yeah." My brow furrowed. "I don't get it."

Then I got it.

Could it be that "Rooster" was servicing more than the lawns of all the old "hens" in the neighborhood?

I grimaced. "Hey Winky, ever heard the figure of speech, 'I'll never be able to unsee that,'?"

Winky grinned. "Yep."

"Turns out it works for things you only see with your *mind's* eye, too."

Winky groaned. "You had to go there, didn't you."

Winky and I were about to drive out of the trailer park when I spotted Geraldine's old Ford. It stuck out like a rusty thumb among the small cluster of beige and silver sedans parked in front of the Queen of the Road clubhouse.

Even though I had a lot on my plate, I just had to know what Geraldine was doing.

"Winky! Pull the van into the parking lot. Let's see what Geraldine's up to."

"You got it, Chief!" Winky grinned deviously. "Watch this!"

Winky swerved into the clubhouse parking lot on two wheels. He rocketed into a parking space beside a dumpster, slammed on the brakes, and cut the van's ignition. Before I could even bob back to sitting upright, he'd hopped out of the driver's seat.

"What the?" I muttered as I watched through the windshield as Winky zigzagged across the lawn like a fugitive dodging bullets. When he reached an eight-foot-tall juniper tree the size and shape of a Christmas tree, he stopped. Sidling his back up against it, he waved for me to join him.

I sighed, climbed out of the van, and walked over to him. "We don't have to be sneaky, Winky. We're not doing anything illegal. We're just ... you know ... looking around."

Winky's left eyebrow flatlined. "Lookin' around? You forget who we're dealing with? Ms. Geraldine Jiggles might not take too kindly to you spying on her."

"But I'm not—"

The words died in my mouth. Winky was right. I actually *was* spying on Geraldine—sort of. I mean, what other excuse could I give for being here at the clubhouse, or even in her trailer park, for that matter?

My nose crinkled. "You're right. Let's get out of here."

"Aww, no stakeout?" Winky's face crumbled like a stomped saltine cracker. "Why not?"

"Because—"

Suddenly the door to the clubhouse flew open. Two elderly women came rushing out. One was Sylvia, the lady with the silver bun! I dived back behind the bush, dragging Winky with me.

"Shh!" I hissed, putting a finger to my lips.

"I can't believe they're not going to do anything about that pervert!" I heard Sylvia say to the other woman as they passed by us on the sidewalk. "What good is an HOA if the board is just a bunch of namby-pambies?"

"Ugh!" the red-haired woman said. "It's gotten to where a woman's dignity is a thing of the past. The nerve of the man! Spying on us like that!"

Winky's pudgy face registered sheer panic. "How'd they spot me, Val?"

"Hush!" I hissed. "I don't think they're talking about you."

"Then who?"

My face puckered. "It's gotta be *Rooster.*"

"Ha!" Winky laughed, then clapped his hand over his own mouth. He leaned in and whispered in my ear, "Like my Grammy used to say, 'Whistling girls and crowin' hens both shall come to no good end.'"

My nose crinkled. "What's that got to do with anything?"

Winky scratched his head. "How am I supposed to know? Grammy's the one what said it."

"Ugh. Can it already!" I whispered, watching as both women got on their bicycles. As they pedaled away, I shook my head. "Somebody's definitely up to no good around here. It sounds like they're having a meeting about it inside the clubhouse right now. Let's slip around the back and see if there's a place we can listen in where they can't see us."

Winky's eyes grew wide. "You mean like a stakeout?"

"Argh! Okay, sure. It's a stakeout. But just a really short one. Then I need to get back to Belated Rooms and set up my shop."

"And make that call to Shirley Saurwein," Winky said.

I blew out a sigh. "Ugh. Don't remind me."

• • • •

FROM BEHIND THE COVER of a beach towel slung over the back of a pool lounger, Winky and I, on hands and knees, took turns sneaking surreptitious peeks past the pool and into the open sliding glass doors of the clubhouse.

In the dim, greenish light of the overhead fluorescents, I made out the shadowy figures of three women sitting around a rectangular table.

"How much chlorine you think a pool like this uses?" Winky asked, poking me from behind.

"Hush!" I hissed. "I'm trying to hear what they're saying!"

"Good thing they all got on hearin' aids," Winky said.

"What?" I grumbled, shifting my aching knees on the pool deck's merciless concrete pavers. "How do you know they're wearing hearing aids?"

"Makes 'em talk loud," Winky said. "My Aunt Vera wore 'em. I swear you could hear that woman jabberin' over a space shuttle launch."

"Shhh!" I hissed again. "If you don't keep quiet, *you're* gonna need a miracle, and it won't be for your ear!"

I leaned forward, cupped a hand behind my right ear, and strained to hear the voices emanating from inside the clubhouse.

"Thank goodness you found new sponsors, Geraldine," I heard a woman with a New Jersey accent say. "But now we've got an even bigger problem."

"What now?" Geraldine grumbled. It was her, all right. I could recognize her distinctive gravelly voice anywhere.

"Dan the Dancing Harmonica Man can't make it," a third woman with a high-pitched voice said. "He blew a gasket at the hoedown last Saturday night. He's scheduled for hernia surgery tomorrow."

"Dang it!" Geraldine hissed. "He was supposed to be our big event! This is my first year as the fair's sponsor. We need to make a bigger splash than that deadbeat Orville Ledbetter was going to. Come on, gals. Think of something!"

"We need a main event," the Jersey woman said. "A pièce de résistance, if you will."

"Oh! I've got it!" the third, high-pitched voice said. "My nephew, Gary! He did the opening at the Survivalist Fair at Dreadmore Village last year."

"Dreadmore Village?" Geraldine asked. "That fancy place near Lakeland?"

"The very same!" the third woman said.

"Sounds expensive," Geraldine said. "How much does he charge, Helga?"

"For me?" Helga said, her high voice bursting with pride. "He'd do it for free."

"Free, huh?" Geraldine said. "Was anyone arrested during his show?"

"What?" Helga said. "Certainly not!"

"How about after?" Geraldine asked.

"No!"

"Good. Book him," Geraldine said.

I heard something hit the table. It sounded like a judge's mallet. "Next order of business?" Geraldine said.

"I was thinking we could—" Helga said.

"Hold it!" Geraldine yelled over her.

I peeked out from behind the towel. Curling both hands to form binoculars against the blinding sun, I took a gander through the club-house's open doors and nearly swallowed my tonsils. Geraldine was staring out the door directly at me.

"Goggles!" she yelled and jumped up from the table.

Instantly, the other two women joined her. The trio of surly seniors scrambled through the glass doors before Winky and I could even get up off of our knees. From the looks on their faces, the only thing they forgot to bring with them were flaming pitchforks.

"Val? What are *you* doing here?" Geraldine bellowed.

I smiled up at her lamely. "Um ... Winky and I came to see if we could help out with the fair."

"From behind a pool lounger?" Helga asked. "That's highly irregular!"

"We didn't want to interrupt your meeting," I said, standing up and brushing off the knees of my jeans.

"We was just admiring your pool area," Winky said.

Helga gasped. "Not *another* one!"

"Beg your pardon?" Winky asked.

"You came here to *help* us?" Geraldine asked, her voice tinged with more than just a dab of suspicion.

"Yes. With the pool area," I blurted. "We thought we could make it nice for the fair." I elbowed my partner in crime. "Isn't that right, Winky?"

Winky nodded. "Sure. I mean, I got me a donut and fishin' bait shop down at the beach. I sell donut floaties. They's purty popular. If'n you want, I could bring a bunch of 'em to put in the pool for decoration. You know, long as you don't mind 'em havin' my logo on 'em and all."

"Oh. I guess that'd be all right," Helga said. "As long as that's *all* they'll have on them."

"And you'll do it for free," Jersey woman said.

Geraldine eyed me. "You came all the way over here to talk to me about decorating the pool area? You could've called."

"We wanted to ... assess what we were working with," I said.

"Uh-huh." Geraldine folded her arms across her scrawny chest. "So, did you call Saurwein and get that ad space for Saturday?"

"It's on my list for as soon as we get back," I said.

I wasn't lying. Given the look on Geraldine's face, I knew I'd better keep my word. Otherwise, she'd throw me headfirst into the deep end—without a donut of the eating *or* floating kind.

Chapter Ten

Winky and I cruised down Corey Avenue in his old blue van, a dilapidated rocking chair strapped to the roof like a remake of *The Beverly Hillbillies*. We had to. Inside, the van was packed to the ceiling with all the junk I'd bought off "Rooster" the riding-mower guy.

"Geez. I hope I haven't blown it with Geraldine," I said as we pulled up in front of Belated Rooms. "I shouldn't have gone to her clubhouse. But … I just wanted to make sure she and the other ladies at the trailer park were safe from that weirdo, Rooster."

"You ain't foolin' me, Val-Pal," Winky said, wagging his ginger eyebrows at me. "Come on. What was we *really* spyin' on her for?"

I frowned. "Fine. I wanted to make sure she wasn't packing up and heading to Vegas with the money I gave her for the fair sponsorship. She's an avid slots player, in case you didn't know." I shook my head. "Winky, I can't have her blowing that $4500. It's all the money I have!"

"I thought you two was supposed to be trusting each other."

Winky opened the van door while I unhooked my seatbelt.

"I'm trying to," I said. "But I've already been the unwitting victim of her sketchy plans on more than one occasion."

Winky chuckled. "Aww, you heard what them clubhouse ladies said. Geraldine already gave 'em the money. So quit worryin'. She's just a harmless little old lady trying to make a livin' just like the rest of us."

I frowned. "I know. You're probably right." I climbed out of the passenger seat and followed Winky to the back of the van. "But I've got a lot more riding on this besides the money."

"Like what?" Winky asked, pulling open the van's back door.

"You know that roll of quarters I thought I saw in her purse?"

"Yep."

"It turns out it was a gun!" I shook my head. "Hot-headed Geraldine is walking around with a weird old revolver in her bag. She's already got a hair-trigger temper. What if she's got a hair-trigger finger as well?"

Winky scoffed as he sorted through the boxes of junk we'd bought off Rooster. "Lots a people tote guns nowadays. She's pro'lly just practicing for that Pokemon shootout at the fair."

"The Shootout at the Poke Corral," I corrected. My left eyebrow flatlined. "Wait a minute. How did *you* know Geraldine plans on participating in that?"

Winky plucked a toaster from one of the boxes and examined a suspicious round hole in its side. "Just a lucky guess?" He put the toaster back in the box and shot me a *father-knows-best* look.

"Now quit worryin' about the fair," he said. "*You*, young lady, had best get on the horn right now and call that reporter woman a'fore you end up starring as the bullseye in Geraldine's next target practice."

I grimaced. "I don't know which woman is deadlier, Geraldine or Saurwein."

Winky laughed. "Stop 'crastinatin' all ready. Tell you what. I'll unload this stuff while you make that call."

"Fine," I grumbled. "But I swear, Winky. Some days even procrastination seems like too much work."

· · · ·

"YOU WANT A HALF-PAGE ad in Saturday's edition?" Saurwein asked over the phone, then laughed so loudly I had to move the speaker away from my ear. "That's *the day after tomorrow*. Too bad, Fremden. The production files got sent to the printers hours ago."

"Can't you stop them?" I pleaded. "Otherwise Geraldine said she was going to post flyers with pictures of us all over the fair."

I heard Saurwein gasp. "Not the pictures of us at—"

"*Yes. Those* pictures. And she'll do it, too. Believe me!"

"Gawd! And I thought *my* boss was horrible."

"You have no idea. Please! I'm begging you. Can't you just take something out of the issue and replace it with information about the survivalist fair?"

"What information are we talking about?"

"I dunno."

"Seriously? Are you out of your mind, Fremden?"

"Wait. I know! You could use the poster artwork. I've got it on my laptop."

"Argh! Email me the file," Saurwein grumbled. "I'll see what I can do."

"Thanks. And ... um ... any chance you could mention the grand opening of my shop, *Simply Smashing*?"

"Are you kidding? You should be grateful I don't 'simply smash' your face in the next time I see you."

I grimaced. "Fair enough. I owe you one."

"Oh, I'd say that's the understatement of the century. If I pull this off, you owe me exclusive access for interviews with the fair's main headliners. Got it?"

"Got it."

"Good. Now let me go and try to fix this crazy mess before it's too late!"

Saurwein clicked off the phone. I rushed over to my laptop and emailed the poster file to her. That done, I sucked in an anxious breath. Hopefully my latest attempt to avoid disaster wouldn't develop into a whole new one.

While I chewed my thumbnail to the quick, the front door to the thrift shop squeaked open. I looked up to see Winky hauling in the old rocking chair that'd been strapped to the roof of his van ala *The Beverly Hillbillies*.

"This is the last of it," he said, grinning at me. "Come take a look."

"At what?"

He winked and hitched up his droopy jeans. "You'll see."

I followed Winky as he shuffled past tables of not-gently-used underpants and worn-out household junk. He stopped and set the rocking chair down under the banner announcing my new shop, Simply Smashing.

"Go ahead on in," he said, motioning toward the door.

I stepped inside. My mouth fell open. While I'd been haggling on the phone with Saurwein, Winky had set up my place.

On the wall beside the entrance, six shiny new hammers hung on hooks, along with four pairs of used mechanics coveralls. Along the walls and in every corner, "smashing stations" heaped high with tempting junk sat begging to be whacked to smithereens.

"How did you do all this?" I asked.

Winky shrugged. "I guess owning the donut and bait shop has gone and turned me into a bona fide merchandising genius."

I grinned. "That's for sure!" I hugged him. "How can I ever thank you?"

"Like I said before, just *don't* make me eat no dinner you fixed and we're square."

I laughed. "Deal. Tell you what. I'll meet you bright and early Saturday at the trailer park clubhouse. I'll help you get your stuff set up in the pool area in time for the fair."

Winky beamed. "Thanky. What with Winnie havin' to stay and run our shop, I could use a hand."

"Oh," I added. "And don't forget the donuts!"

"Which ones? The eatin' kind or the floatin' kind?"

I smirked. "Why can't it be both?"

Winky grinned. "I like your style, Val-Pal. I like your style."

Chapter Eleven

"You're my hero," I said, my voice rusty from sleep.

    I sat up in bed, rubbed my eyes, and took the cappuccino Tom was offering. He shot me a smile even hotter than the steaming coffee in my cup.

"What kind of mischief are you up to today?" he asked, his sea-green eyes sparkling.

"I'm having a trial run of Simply Smashing at noon. Don't you remember?"

"Oh, yeah." Tom leaned over and gave me a kiss. "Seems I do recall something about that." He pulled a gift bag from behind his back and handed it to me. "A little something to get your new business off with a bang."

"Really?" I squealed, setting the cappuccino on the nightstand. I grabbed the bag, reached into it, and pulled out a gleaming silver hammer. I smirked. "I think you may know me too well."

"I do," he winked. "And I love you anyway."

• • • •

AFTER TOM LEFT, I'D washed down a Pop Tart with a second cappuccino. Then, in an effort to conduct myself in a more professional manner, on the drive over to Belated Rooms, I'd taken another peek inside Milly's binder full of rules for success. The first one read:

1. Arrive on time, and with a smile.

I glanced at the time on my cell phone. It was nearly 10 a.m.

Well, it's too late for the first part, but I can still do the second.

I pulled Shabby Maggie into a parking space and pasted on a smile. As I headed inside the shop, I spotted Geraldine at the cash register, her back to me. She was talking to somebody on the shop's landline phone.

"I need this done ASAP," she said. "If you don't take care of it by the weekend, I'll take matters into my own hands!" She slammed the receiver down in the cradle and sighed. "Seems like it's you and me against the world, Barney. You're the only one I could ever count on."

My pasted-on smile came unglued.

Nice. So much for our partnership of trust.

"Who's Barney?" I asked.

Geraldine gasped. I'd obviously startled her. She whirled around to face me. "None of your dang business, that's who!"

"Geez! Sorry!" I said, holding up my palms. "I didn't mean to pry."

The last thing I wanted was to start the first day of my new business on a sour note. I mustered a smile I hoped would sweeten Geraldine's mood. "Hey, would you like to participate in the trial run today? The first whack is on the house!"

Geraldine's beady eyes darted around the thrift shop. "You better not be whacking anything in *my* house!" She grabbed her purse from under the checkout counter. "Mind the store. I'm outta here."

I blanched. "But ... where are you ... I mean, why are you leaving?"

"I don't wanna hear all the racket!" Geraldine shuffled out from behind the plexiglass counter, her green Crocs slapping dully on the scuffed linoleum floor.

"It shouldn't be that loud," I said. "Besides, the trial run isn't until noon."

"It's already past ten," Geraldine grumbled. "I've been waiting for you so I can go take care of some business with the fair."

"Oh."

Geraldine tucked her cellphone into the breast pocket of her polyester shirt. Its loud tropical print made my eyes swim. "I'm serious, Fremden!" she yelled.

My nose crinkled. "Serious about what?"

"Don't let anybody bust up my merchandise while I'm gone!" She glanced over at the ancient black cash register as big as a mini fridge.

"Especially that old thing. It's worth more than anything else in this whole place."

"Okay, okay!" I said. "I'll make sure nobody damages any of your fine merchandise."

"You'd better." Geraldine headed for the front door, then stopped and turned around. "Did you call Saurwein?"

I puffed out my chest. "Yes. I did. The ad comes out in tomorrow's Saturday edition."

Geraldine scowled. "How about the liability insurance? The last thing we need is to get sued over your silly smashing shenanigans."

"Milly says we're covered, as long as we take the required precautions for customer safety. I've got the heavy-duty coveralls, the gloves, the helmets, the—"

"What about protective eyewear?"

"Yes," I said as the shop door suddenly squeaked open. "I've got goggles taken care of, so stop worrying!"

"Um, hello?" Davy Eber said as he walked into the shop.

"Oh. Hi, Davy," I said. "What's up?"

Davy shot me a sheepish look. "Just seeing if you needed me to do anything else for the shootout at the Poke Corral."

"Anything else?" I asked.

"He's doing the announcements during the shootout," Geraldine said.

"Along with some antique gun trivia thrown in," Davy added.

"Oh." I smiled. "That sounds interesting."

Geraldine rolled her eyes and headed for the door. "I've heard his spiel before. I've got better things to do."

"Well, have a nice day," Eber said to Geraldine's backside as it disappeared out the door. He sighed. "Well, I guess I'll get back to my shop."

"Wait a second," I said. "I want to talk to you about Geraldine."

He smiled wistfully. "That woman's a real pistol, isn't she."

"Funny you should say that. Have you seen hers?"

Eber blanched. "Her what?"

"Geraldine's *pistol*. The loaded one she keeps in her purse?"

"Oh." Eber nodded. "Well, of course I've seen it. I sold it to her. It's a beauty, isn't it? A .38 special. That model was the regular carry for policemen back in the 1930s."

My nose crinkled. "What would Geraldine need with a gun like that?"

"She's old school, like me." Eber grinned. "We like to keep the memory of the good old days alive."

I sighed. "Well, that would certainly explain why she seems hell bent on sending me back to the Great Depression."

Chapter Twelve

Just like the impending Shootout at the Poke Corral, I, too, had a date with destiny at high noon.

At 12 o'clock on the dot, the door to the thrift shop squeaked open and my first customer came bustling in. My choice hadn't been left to chance. In fact, she didn't even know about it. But I figured if I could win over this prim and proper diva as a customer, the sky was the limit for Simply Smashing.

"You made it!" I said as my perfectly coifed and manicured best friend came bustling through the door, her arms laden with shopping bags.

"Sorry if I'm late for our lunch date, Val," Milly said. "I fired Shirley Saurwein right before I left. That woman doesn't go down without a fight."

I grimaced. "Tell me something I *don't* know."

Milly beamed her gorgeous smile my way. "Oh, forget her. This is *your* day. Just wait till you see what I've got for you!"

"Um ... what's with the fancy shopping bags? I thought you were going to stick to the budget I gave you."

"Silly you!" Milly gushed. "I couldn't let my bestie start her new adventure wearing some cheap, ill-fitting outfit! Here, take these."

Milly shoved half a dozen gift bags into my hands. "These are your new uniform," she said. "I found the cutest pink T-shirts and overalls. And a pink headband and matching pink tennis shoes!"

"Sounds like a lot of pink," I said.

"Oh, no. There's never too much pink." Milly shooed me toward the back of the shop. "Quick! Go try them on in the ladies' room!"

I gave in to her indulgence and grinned. "Okay, already!" I squealed, then scurried into the washroom.

After stripping off my old mom jeans and stretched-out T-shirt, I peeked inside the first bag. I pulled out a pair of overalls one size too small. I sighed. Then I remembered the rule: When it came to buying a woman clothes, it was always better to go too small than too large. You could take clothes back, but not hurt feelings.

I tried on the overalls and was delighted when they actually fit! Instantly in a good mood, I slipped on the pink shirt, headband, and pink tennis shoes. Everything fit like a glove. I smiled. It seems my best friend knew me both inside *and* out.

Feeling like a half-million bucks, I emerged from the washroom. Milly was standing there beaming at me like a bridesmaid inspecting her bestie's wedding gown.

"Oh, Val. You look great! As rule number three says, *Dress for the part you want.*"

"Well, what I want *right now* is to give you a hug."

"Bring it in," Milly said, raising her arms and rushing toward me. We hugged each other tight.

"And now I'd like to return the favor," I said, pulling back from her embrace.

"What do you mean?"

"I want you to be the first one to test out my new form of retail therapy."

Milly glanced up at the Simply Smashing banner. "You mean ..."

"Yep! Come with me." I took Milly by the hand and led her to the door of my little shop. "Oh. Did you get the goggles?"

"I did." Milly held up the last bag, still in her hand. "They're in here."

"Good." I took the bag, reached in, and handed Milly a pair of goggles. Then I took a pair for myself. After putting them on, I handed Milly a helmet and a hammer, then opened the door to Simply Smashing.

"Milly, I want *you* to christen my new business."

"Me?"

"Yes, you!" I nudged her through the door. "Just take your hammer and whack anything inside the shop."

Milly blinked. "Anything?"

I nodded. "Anything."

Milly glanced around worriedly at the assortment of junk Winky had assembled into "whacking stations." She bit her lower lip. "I don't know, Val. I might break something."

I laughed. "That's the whole idea."

Her cute nose crinkled. "Are you sure?"

"Yes, I'm sure."

Milly took a tentative step into the shop. She stopped in front of a chipped bunny statue about two feet tall. She turned back and gave me a childlike, doe-eyed stare. "I want you to know this goes against everything my mother taught me."

I grinned. "Just pretend that rabbit statue is Shirley Saurwein."

Milly pursed her lips with determination, then gingerly tapped the ugly garden statue with her hammer. "Take that," she said softly.

"Harder," I said.

Milly glanced up at me. "You know, when I was a kid, my cousin Joey used to tell me *Peter Cottontail* was going to come and steal all my Easter candy."

I stifled a giggle. "Did he?"

"Yes." Milly frowned. "But now I think it might've been Joey who took my candy all along."

I smirked. "How about pretending that bunny is Joey."

Milly's eyes grew wide. She stared down at the doomed ceramic rabbit. "You jerk!" she squealed as her hammer came down hard on the bunny's head, sending one of its ears flying.

"Now that's more like it," I said.

Milly turned to me, her blue eyes gleaming. "OMG!"

I smiled like a drug dealer. "I know. Isn't it wonderful?"

I was about to tell her to hit it again, but I didn't have to. Without warning, Milly began to beat that poor, ugly bunny statue to a pulp. When its head splintered, she grinned over at me like Charlie Manson, then moved on to an old ashtray. As her hammer went down and shattered it to pieces, I ducked for cover and slipped out of the room.

I watched five minutes tick off on the old cat clock on the wall. Apparently, Joey wasn't the only one who'd wronged my best friend. Finally, the sound of shattering glass and crunching metal abated. The door to Simply Smashing slowly opened. Milly emerged looking exhausted but serene, as if she'd just returned from a five-week stay at a health retreat.

"Val! I had no idea this could be so ... fantastically therapeutic!" she said between ragged breaths.

I grinned. "Why else do you think *I* do it?"

Milly's ecstatic expression skipped a beat. "Um ..."

"You don't have to answer that," I said sourly, then gently took the hammer from her trembling hand.

"Val, I didn't mean—"

"We all have our reasons to be frustrated," I said. "Rule number one at my shop is: *Don't ask, don't tell.*'"

Milly nodded and removed her helmet. "Thanks."

I smiled. "No worries. Now, as my first customer, I have a brief survey. What did you think of the variety of junk on offer? Anything you'd add or subtract?"

"No. It was perfect, Val. Simply perfect."

I pursed my lips. "Was it ugly enough? I figured the uglier the junk, the better. I mean, the less appealing something is, the more you want to smash it, right?"

Milly grinned. "Absolutely! Anybody who's ever dated knows that!"

I laughed. "You ready to go to lunch now?"

Milly eyed the hammer in my hand. "Sure. Just give me one more minute. I forgot about Harvey." She put the helmet back on her head, snatched the hammer from my hand, and made a beeline back toward Simply Smashing.

"Oh," she called out as she slipped inside, "If you ever want a franchise partner, just let me know!"

Chapter Thirteen

I t was the morning of the fair, and the news wasn't good. *Literally.* As I sipped my first cappuccino in bed, Tom returned carrying a copy of the Saturday edition of the *Beach Gazette*.

"This was on the driveway," he said. "Along with a fresh pair of skid marks. What's going on?"

"Saurwein," I muttered, as if the words tasted bad in my mouth. "Gimme that."

I took the paper from Tom and unfolded it. To my shock and surprise, Saurwein had kept her promise. She'd put the ad for the fair on the front page. But Saurwein being Saurwein, she couldn't do anything without getting a dig in edgewise.

She'd run the image of the poster, along with a dubious headline that read:

> *Survivalist Fair Barely Survives Loss of Long-Time Sponsor.*
> *Jiggles Wiggles In.*

I sighed.

Great. Geraldine is gonna love that.

I quickly scanned the rest of the article. It appeared accurate in every detail—except one. I'd been the one who'd put up the cash to save the fair, but Saurwein hadn't mentioned my name once.

"Figures." I tossed the paper onto the bed beside me.

"What figures?" Tom asked, pulling on a pair of socks.

Outside, a horn honked, saving me the trouble of explaining. I leapt out of bed and peeked out between the miniblinds. "Oh, crap. I'm running late. Winky's here already! We're setting up the pool for the fair this morning. Stall him while I get ready. Please?"

"I'm meeting J.D. for a round of golf in thirty minutes," Tom said. "But I can spare a second." He laughed and wrapped his arms around me. "What's in it for *me*?"

I kissed him lightly on the lips, then pulled free and made a mad dash for my closet. "Winky should be packing a huge stash of donuts."

Tom laughed. "Cop kryptonite. How can I resist that?"

I grinned. "Good luck with your golf game. What's J.D.'s handicap?"

"Besides the fact that he's married to Laverne?" Tom quipped.

"J.D.'s barely four feet tall in heels," I said.

"Maybe. But being short doesn't slow him down one bit. The man can still swing a mean club."

I smirked. "Think he'd be interested in swinging a hammer, too?"

"Careful," Tom said with a wink. "Your businesswoman is showing."

• • • •

ON A MISSION TO TURN the pool into a donut-riddled paradise, Winky and I pulled into the clubhouse at Queen of the Road Trailer Park ready for action. The parking lot was already half full of vehicles. In the grassy area surrounding the clubhouse and pool, vendors were busy setting up their booths for the fair.

Amid the chaos, I heard an engine's roar. I glanced around and spotted someone atop a riding mower. He was wearing a straw hat. I squinted against the sun's glare. "Is that Rooster?"

"I'd bet dollars to donuts on it," Winky said, hitching a thumb toward the back of the van. "And today, I'm packin'."

My freckled friend wasn't kidding. The entire van was stacked three feet deep in donut boxes and deflated donut floats.

"Hey! Let's see if Rooster needs a donut," Winky said.

My nose crinkled. "The floating kind or the eating kind?"

Winky grinned. "Don't matter to me."

Winky parked his old blue van in a spot beside the grass adjacent to where Rooster was mowing. When his noisy riding mower got close enough, Winky waved him over.

"What're you doing mowing this morning?" I asked. "I thought you did the whole place on Thursday."

"I was supposed to," Rooster said. He patted the riding mower's steering wheel. "But this old gal kept sputtering out. Took a day to find a new carburetor. It put me behind, but not to worry. I should be done before the fair starts."

"Have you a donut," Winky said, shoving an open box at him. "We got lots a donuts to blow up a'fore the big shindig."

Rooster eyed the box of sweet treats with mock suspicion. "Not any of these, I hope?"

"He means donut *floats*," I said. "We have to blow them up for the pool. We're making a little celebration station here for the folks participating in the Shootout at the Poke Corral."

"Cool," Rooster said. "What time is that gonna be?"

"High noon, a course," Winky said.

"Geez, it's almost ten." Rooster grabbed a donut. "I better get a move on."

"Us, too," I said.

Rooster looked me up and down, then winked. "Well, good luck," he said. "Hope everything goes off without a bang!"

· · · ·

THE POOL WAS HALF FILLED with donut floaties when Geraldine came skittering out of the clubhouse like her skunk hair was on fire. Given the fact that her entire outfit was made of plastic and polyester, if she'd actually been aflame, she'd have melted before she made it to the pool deck.

"Quick!" the old lady hollered. "I got a job for you!"

I blanched with surprise. For once, Geraldine's cranky belligerence wasn't aimed at me. She was looking at Winky.

"What's a matter?" Winky asked.

Geraldine grabbed him by the arm. "One of the toilets is overflowing! Can you fix it?"

"Prolly," Winky said. "That's one a my specialties. Besides makin' donuts, that is."

"You come too, Fremden," Geraldine said. "I need you on mop patrol."

Dang it. I thought I was in the clear. Talk about a crappy way to start the day ...

. . . .

"THAT WAS AN EASY ONE," Winky said, rinsing his hands in the ladies' room sink. "The inflow tube in the tank come a'loose. It's workin' good as new now."

"All I can say is, thank god the water was *clean*," I said as I squeezed the mophead out into the janitor bucket.

Geraldine gave the toilet a trial flush. "It all seems back in order." She looked up at us. "What? You two get back to work!"

Before Winky and I could close our gaping mouths, Geraldine hustled us out of the washroom. Once we were back outside in the pool area, she seemed to calm down.

"Your friend here's pretty handy," Geraldine said, patting Winky on the back. "And Fremden, you did a good job with that ad in the *Beach Gazette*." She glanced around the pool area. "The pool looks pretty good, too."

I studied her carefully. "Have you switched medications recently?"

"What?" Geraldine grumbled. Her cell phone rang, saving me from the consequences of my quip.

"Aww, crap!" Geraldine said, staring at the phone display. "One problem solved and another one springs up."

"What now?" Winky asked.

"I need someone to fill in at the shootout. Orville Ledbetter didn't show up!"

"Oooh!" Winky jumped up and down, then raised his hand. "I can do it! Purty please?"

Geraldine eyed him up and down. "You got a gun?"

Winky's excitement disappeared like a cat with a hot fish stick. "No ma'am. Not on me."

Geraldine pursed her lips. "No matter. Davy should have an extra. You'll have to do."

"Hot dawg!" Winky hooted. "When do you need me?"

"The shootout starts in less than an hour. I've got a lot of release forms you need to sign first. Come with me."

Winky glanced over at me. "But—"

"It's okay, Winky," I said shooing him off with a smile. "I can finish up here. I'll meet you there in half an hour. Good luck!"

• • • •

TWENTY MINUTES LATER, the pool area looked magnificent. The entire surface of the water was jam-packed with Winky's realistic-looking donut floats, each covered in brightly printed frosting and sprinkles. At the far end of the pool, the tiki hut was crammed with *real* donuts.

Unfortunately, so was my belly. I was a sucker for a crème-filled.

Flying high on a sugar buzz, I grabbed my purse, intent on making my way over to the Shootout at the Poke Corral. But as I closed the pool gate behind me, I was accosted by the sound of a familiar, sarcastic voice.

"Don't forget, Fremden. You owe me," Saurwein said, shaking her finger in my face. She peered at me from underneath a floppy beach hat. "It wasn't easy to get you that ad in the *Beach Gazette*. I had to delete one of our regular customers to fit it in."

I turned to face her. "Gee, how can I ever thank you?"

The bottle blonde stopped cracking her chewing gum mid chew. "Don't get smart. You *should* be thanking me. The editor would have my head if she knew I'd cut Looker's Eyewear to run your stupid fair poster."

"Then why—"

"Eh," Saurwein shrugged. "The old geezer probably won't even notice. Anyway, now it's *your* turn to pony up the goods. You owe me exclusive access to interview the shootout participants."

"Fine by me." As I locked the gate behind me, I wondered what the big deal was. "Why do you care about a stupid little fair like this one anyway?"

"If you wanna get ahead as a journalist, you need *drama*," Saurwein said.

"Drama?" I asked, side-stepping an anthill as we picked our way through a strip of tall grass by the pool on our way to the shootout.

"You should know this by now, Fremden. In Florida, if you wanna get published, gunfire is practically a *requirement*."

"But not the *correct name* of a financial sponsor," I said sourly.

Saurwein smiled cruelly. "You saw the article, eh?"

"Yeah. And I don't appre—"

"Oo-la-la!" Saurwein said, ignoring me. "Speaking of articles, that guy over there could make an interesting one."

I glanced over in that direction. Rooster was on his riding mower, making quick work of the last bit of lawn. I laughed. "Ha. You're in luck, Saurwein. You're just his type."

Saurwein wagged her eyebrows. "Smart?"

"Nope. *Desperate*."

"Ha ha," Saurwein hissed. "At least I wasn't desperate enough to sign up for the dunking booth."

"There's a dunking booth?"

"Yeah. Isn't that your friend over there? That scuzzy lawyer?"

"Finkerman?"

I glanced to my left. At the end of a row of port-o-potties stood an old-fashioned carnival dunking booth. Sitting in the hotseat, above a pool of Ty D Bol blue water, was my old friend/nemesis, Ferrol Finkerman.

"With that fuzzy orange hair and ridiculous outfit, what's he supposed to be? A homeless clown?" Saurwein asked.

I didn't have the heart to tell her that was the way Finkerman always looked. Unable to resist the lure of an easy mark, I sprinted over to the booth.

"Hiya, Finkerman," I said. "Fancy meeting you here."

Through the cage wire, I saw his Adam's apple bob up and down on his skinny turkey neck.

"Oh, crap. It's you," he said.

I grinned like a psycho killer "It is!" I turned to the old man running the booth. "What's it cost to throw?"

"Three bucks a ball," he said. "Or three balls for six bucks."

I pulled out a fiver. It was all I had. "Saurwein," I yelled as she walked up. "Can I borrow a dollar? It's an emergency."

She frowned. "I thought we were going to the shootout. It's just about to start."

I stared at her like she was nuts. "You don't expect me to miss the opportunity of a lifetime, do you?"

Saurwein took a gander at Finkerman. "No, I guess not." She pulled out her wallet and handed me a dollar. "But *I* get one of the balls."

"Not a chance." I handed over the money and grabbed a softball.

"Prepare to meet your doom," I yelled at Finkerman.

"Kill me now," he muttered, then hunkered down and closed his eyes.

I reared back, but just as I made my throw, a gunshot rang out. I fumbled and missed the target.

"Crap on a cracker," I yelled.

"Dang it, Fremden!" Saurwein yelled. "Come on! We're missing the shootout!"

"But I've got two balls left!" I whined.

"That's two more than the guy in the booth has," Saurwein said. "Let me show you how it's done."

Saurwein snatched a softball from my hand and whirled it Finkerman's way. It smacked the target dead on. Finkerman went down with the ship like a drowning rat.

"Come on," Saurwein said, grabbing my arm and dragging me along before I had a chance to throw the last ball.

"Dang it," I grumbled.

I guess Glad was right. Sometimes you just have to get your jollies vicariously.

Chapter Fourteen

In Florida, when it came to getting people to leave the sanctum of their air-conditioned domiciles, no combination worked faster than random gunfire and the potential for disaster. So, it stood to reason that when that first shot rang out at the survivalist fair, nobody ran faster toward the sound of the blast than yours truly.

The gunshot's echo had barely faded before Saurwein and I took off, leaving poor, soaked-to-the-skin Finkerman to dunk another day. We'd barely made it 50 feet through the crowd when a second gunshot rang out.

I stopped, frozen in my tracks. Not because of the gunshot, but because I'd been blindsided by what lay straight in front of me.

Just on the other side of the concrete block wall that surrounded the trailer park, a mountain of dirt and trash loomed halfway up the sky like a gigantic garbage tsunami. Hundreds of seagulls soared in the sky above it. Atop the mound sat a yellow dump truck. It looked like a toy in comparison.

I blinked at it blankly. How had I not noticed this before? Queen of the Road Trailer Park sat butt-to-cheek with the only kind of mountain we had in Florida. In other words, the trailer park's next-door neighbor was the county dump.

"Well, that explains the smell," Saurwein said. "I thought it was your new cologne, *Eau de Clogged Toilette*."

"Ha ha." Before I could conjure up my own sarcastic comeback, a third gunshot rang out.

I clawed my eyes away from Mount Trashmore. In the distance, I spotted four archery-style targets set up along the concrete retaining wall. A sizeable crowd had gathered around.

"The shootout!" I yelled and took off in that direction. I got there just in time to hear an announcement being broadcast over speakers I couldn't see.

"And that concludes the first round. Let's give a hand to Captain Commando," a voice rang out. I recognized it as Davy Eber's.

"Captain Commando?" I muttered over the applause, trying to see over all the people standing around.

"Geez," Saurwein hissed, catching up with me. "If Captain Commando is some troll in assless chaps, I'm gonna barf. I don't get paid enough for this crap."

"At least *you're* getting paid," I grumbled as I worked my way through the crowd.

"Move it," Saurwein said, pushing past me. We wove our way between elbows and armpits up to the line of yellow caution tape holding the spectators clear of the shooting field.

"You've gotta be kidding me," Saurwein said.

"What?" I asked. But one quick glance answered my question. I recognized the first contestant. She was walking away from her target and toward the podium where Eber stood.

Captain Commando was none other than Geraldine Jiggles!

My nose crinkled. Was she ... going commando?

I winced as the unwanted image flashed before my eyes. Yet another I'd never be able to unsee ...

"Next up is Corn Pops," Eber said into the microphone. I saw Geraldine punch him on the arm. "Correction!" Eber said. "Corn Pops has been replaced with ... uh ... let's hear it for *Dough Nut*!"

My nose crinkled. "Dough Nut?"

"I didn't know donuts had freckles," Saurwein quipped.

"Huh?" I spotted Winky shuffling across the grass and yelled, "Go Dough Nut!"

While Winky took position in front of the second target, I ducked under the security tape and ran over to the podium, Saurwein hot on my heels. We arrived to find Eber fighting with Geraldine for control of the mic.

"Please tell me you're wearing underwear," I whispered in Geraldine's ear, causing her to let go of the mic.

"Have you lost it, Fremden?" Geraldine hissed. "I'm *Captain* Commando, not *Going* Commando. There's a difference."

"Thank god," Saurwein said, beating me to it. "But why—"

Geraldine held up her gun. "This little baby is what they call a Junior Commando. It's—"

Suddenly, there was a gunshot blast. Geraldine dropped her gun. "Oh, crap," she said while I patted myself down for bullet holes. Thankfully, there weren't any.

"Geez, Geraldine!" I yelled. "Be careful where you wave that thing!"

She and I both bent over to pick up the gun and ended up knocking heads.

"I'll get it," I grumbled. When I picked up the gun and handed it to her, I noticed her hands were shaking badly. "Are you okay?"

"Yeah," she said. "I'm just old. Nobody tells you rigor mortis starts well before you die."

Before I could laugh, the sound of a second gunshot rang out, followed quickly by a third.

"Well, he didn't take long," Geraldine said, squinting through her bifocals toward Winky's target.

Saurwein sighed. "They never do."

"Let's hear it for Dough Nut!" Eber said over the mic.

The crowd cheered. Winky took a bow, then made a beeline toward us.

Eber raised the mic to his lips again. "Next up is Silver Hammer."

I glanced over at the third target and couldn't believe my eyes. Silver Hammer was Sylvia, the old woman with the silver bun who'd chased Winky and me on her bicycle like the Wicked Witch of the West!

"Well, at least they weren't stupid enough to nickname her Silver Bun," Saurwein quipped.

"Yeah, how dumb would that be," I said as my ears burned.

"Whoa!" Winky said, slapping me on the back. "Good thing ol' Silver Bun wasn't mad at *us* the other day, huh Val-Pal? That woman don't mess around!"

"I knew it," Saurwein said, smirking at me.

I was saved from further humiliation by the sound of three rapid-fire gun blasts. Eber's voice cracked over the mic again. "Let's give it up for Silver Hammer. She really knocked it out of the park!"

As the crowd cheered, Eber put the mic to his lips again. "And now for our final contestant, Randy Dandy!"

A tan, muscular man walked up to the fourth target. He tipped up his straw hat and aimed his gun.

"Rooster is Randy Dandy?" Winky said. He hollered with laughter and wagged his ginger eyebrows at me. "I sure hope his *aim* ain't as accurate as his *nickname*."

"What's he talking about?" Saurwein asked.

I shook my head. "Nothing. Just a dumb joke."

Saurwein shook her head. "Seems like that's the only kind you two know."

Before I could get off my own shot, the next contestant did. True to form, Randy Dandy made quick work of his intended target. Three shots rang out in quick succession.

Blam! Blam! Blam!

"Wow! Let's hear it for Randy Dandy!" Eber announced over the mic. "Well, folks, that concludes the Shootout at the Poke Corral. The scores have been tallied and the winner is ... Dough Nut!"

"Me?" Winky gasped. "Hot dawg!"

"Blast it!" Geraldine grumbled. "That's what I get for letting a young whippersnapper compete."

"I'm fifty-two," Winky said.

Geraldine scoffed. "In our neighborhood, that qualifies you as a teenager."

"And here's your prize," Eber said, handing Winky a slip of paper. "A pass from the Poke Corral food truck for one day of all-you-can-eat sushi!"

"Sushi, eh?" Winky said, so close to the mic that his voice was amplified through the crowd. "Well, that's all right by me, as long as they cook it first."

The crowd roared with laughter.

"Typical Winky," I said, patting him on the back.

"Fremden?" a man's voice sounded behind me. I turned to find police Sergeant McNulty staring down at me through the mirrored lenses of his aviator-style sunglasses. "What are you doing here?"

"Um ... I helped sponsor this thing."

"Really?" His head cocked slightly. "I didn't see any mention of that in the paper."

"Well, you can't believe everything you *don't* read," I said, shooting Saurwein a dirty look. "What are *you* doing here?"

"Security." McNulty glanced around the crowd. "You don't think we let people fire weapons in public without proper precautions, do you?"

"No, sir. Of course not—"

"What in tarnation is that?" I heard Winky holler.

I glanced over to see my freckled friend staring up at the sky like a turkey in the rain. I followed his dumbfounded gaze upward and nearly swallowed my tonsils.

Hovering 20 feet in the air above the crowd was a skinny young man strapped into a lawn chair. Held aloft by a parachute-sized clump of helium balloons, the blond, mullet-haired wonder waved to the crowd.

My nose crinkled. "What the heck?"

McNulty shook his head and sighed. "Why did I move to Florida? *Why?*"

"Is that the second coming of Florida Man?" Winky asked.

"Either that or Moses decided to descend from Mount Trashmore this time," Saurwein said, aiming her phone's camera at the UFO (undignified flying object).

"Wait!" Geradine called out. "That's Gary Wells from Dreadmore Village!"

"She's right! It's me!" the bespectacled, bucktoothed young bean-pole called down to the stunned crowd. "Howdy folks! Thanks for attending the Shootout at the Poke Corral! Now follow me to the clubhouse for the post-shootout celebration!"

As the crowd stared up at him with dumbfounded admiration, Gary pressed a lever on the helium tank poking up between his legs like a silver torpedo. A stream of compressed air shot out, causing his whole makeshift flying contraption to take off in the direction of the clubhouse.

Oohs and *aahs* resounded through the crowd and they began to move in a herd in the same direction as Gary's ingenious redneck flying machine.

As we trailed along, I noticed the sun glinting off something in the sky. It was a fishing line. One end of it was tied to Gary's chair, the other was in the grip of a red-haired woman. She was gently tugging him along like the world's cheapest homemade Macy's Day Parade float.

I quickened my step to catch up with her. But as we turned toward the clubhouse, the red-headed woman tripped on a tree root. Putting her hands out to brace for the fall, she lost her grip on the fishing line. Before she could grab it, a sudden gust of wind caught Gary and blew him and his barrage of balloons right over the pool fence.

"Catch him!" I yelled. But it was too late.

I watched, helpless, as the fishing line snagged on the chain link fence. For a moment, Gary's crazy contraption continued to sail serenely over the pool. But when the snagged line went taut, the lawn chair suddenly jerked to a stop and the balloons kept going. Yanked akimbo, Gary's chair jerked sideways. Suddenly, poor Gary was flailing around like a ... like a ... like a redneck caught in a balloon-propelled lawn chair.

Eager to survive the situation, Gary cut a line and released half of the balloons holding him aloft. As he sunk toward the Earth, he lost his grip on the helium tank between his knees. It splashed down into the pool like a miniature space capsule.

The sudden loss of ballast upturned Gary's chair. The crowd gasped as, for a second, the young man hung upside down, strapped into his chair like a crash-test dummy. Then, like a low-budget remake of the Hindenburg, the whole ridiculous, ill-conceived airship belly-flopped into the pool.

Oh, the humanity.

Gary hit the water, squashing half a dozen of Winky's donut floats to smithereens. All that remained visible of Gary himself was his legs kicking madly like an upturned duck.

"Holy crap!" I screeched, scrambling through the crowd to unlock the pool gate. As I fumbled with the keys, Gary managed to right his chair. I raced to him, relieved to find he was winded, soaked, and surrounded by dead and dying donut floats, but otherwise okay.

Ever the mark of a true professional, Gary rallied enough to wave at the crowd. "I'm okay!" he sputtered.

The crowd cheered and began pouring through the gate toward the pool. I turned to find McNulty was standing right beside me.

"I'm so glad no one was hurt!" I said.

But McNulty wasn't listening. He was staring at the other side of the pool. Suddenly, he took off toward the shallow end. I sprinted after him. When I saw what he saw, my gut dropped four inches.

Inside the center ring of one of Winky's donut floats, a pale, gray face bobbed lazily, staring blindly up at the sky through a pair of swim goggles.

Oh, the humanity, all over again.

Chapter Fifteen

"Everyone stand back!" McNulty shouted.

The crowd, most with their mouths full of donuts, froze. We all stood around the pool, silently ogling, as the police sergeant ran over to the chain-link fence and grabbed a long-handled net hanging near the gate. Then he rushed back to the water's edge.

Kneeling down, McNulty used the net to gently pull the suspicious donut floatie toward the edge of the pool. As it moved ever closer, Mc-Nulty cleared its path, reaching in and plucking out half a dozen of Winky's colorful donut floaties.

As McNulty flung the floats out of the way, the body attached to the bobbing head was revealed.

I could see through the clear water that it belonged to an older white man. Besides the pair of goggles on his head, the hairy, toad-bellied corpse was clad only in a red speedo.

"Aw, hell!" Gary cried out, still floating around in his half-sunk lawn chair. Caught up in a tangle of donut floaties, he tried to paddle his way toward the man with his hands. "I must've crashed into him!" he lamented. "Poor guy couldn't get away fast enough."

Saurwein snorted. "If you ask me, *nobody* in a speedo can get away fast enough."

"You in the lawn chair! Stay back," McNulty ordered.

Gary stopped flapping. The whole crowd grew silent again.

Sergeant McNulty pulled the goggle-wearing man's arm out of the water and tried to take his pulse. We all waited with bated breath.

Finally, McNulty said, "He's dead."

"Oh, no!" Gary whimpered. "I killed him when I dropped the helium tank!"

"Killed who?" Geraldine demanded, pushing her way through the crowd. She spotted the body and hollered, "Good lord! It's Goggles!"

"Someone calm that woman," McNulty said. "She's hysterical."

"She's not hysterical," Sylvia with the silver bun said, leaning forward for a closer look. "Geraldine's right. That's Goggles!"

"Goggles?" McNulty asked.

"Yes." Sylvia glowered at the corpse. "His real name is Orville Ledbetter."

"That popcorn dude?" Winky asked.

"Hush," I whispered, elbowing him. "We've been through this already."

"Oh, lordy!" Winky said, glancing over at the tiki bar. "I better get over there afore they eat me outta house and donuts!"

He took off like a rocket. I glanced up to see the tiki hut had been descended upon by a swarm of grey-haired locusts.

"I'm so sorry," Gary lamented, slapping the water with his hand. "I lost my grip on the helium tank. It was an accident, I swear!"

"No, this was no accident," McNulty said. He draped a beach towel over the body. No longer caught in the floatie, the corpse bobbed freely in the water on the steps of the pool.

Gary groaned. "But I must have—"

"You didn't crash on top of him, and your helium tank wasn't what killed him," McNulty said.

"Then what did?" I asked.

"A bullet," McNulty said. "This man's been shot between the eyes."

Chapter Sixteen

After covering Ledbetter's corpse with a towel, McNulty secured the pool gate and called for backup on his walkie-talkie. Then he stood guard by the gate and announced to the crowd that none of us could leave until more officers arrived and collected our names and contact information.

With nothing better to do while we waited, about 30 of us milled around the pool and clubhouse, exchanging gossip and eating Winky's donuts like starving passengers trapped on a desert isle.

Gary Wells had been salvaged from his ill-fated lounge chair and stood by me draped in a towel, taking savage bites from a frosted cake donut. His appetite appeared to have recovered quickly after learning neither he nor his helium tank had been party to Ledbetter's untimely demise.

"Who's Orville Ledbetter?" Gary asked.

"Good question," McNulty said, glancing over at Geraldine and Sylvia. "Who is he?"

"A resident of the trailer park," Sylvia said, adjusting the bow tied around her silver bun.

"He's also a traitor and a pervert!" Geraldine said, grabbing a chocolate frosted donut from a box lying on the counter of the tiki bar.

From the look on McNulty's face, Geraldine's hostile tone had definitely sparked his interest. "And why would you say that?" he asked.

Geraldine frowned. "He's a dirty old man."

"She's telling the truth!" Sylvia said.

"How so?" McNulty asked.

"We hold a women's aerobics class in the pool three days a week," Geraldine explained. "Orville liked to come down to the pool and watch us ... underwater."

"Gross!" I hissed involuntarily.

"He was a real peeper creeper," Sylvia said. "He'd come to the pool carrying his filthy old gym bag. He'd get out his goggles, put them on, and swim around watching us."

"He never showered first, either, like you're supposed to," a woman with red hair said. I recognized her as the woman who'd used fishing line to tow Gary and his floating chair to the pool. "And let me tell you, that disgusting, greasy hair of his left a nasty oil slick."

"I see there's no love lost between you three and Ledbetter," McNulty said. "I know Ms. Jiggles, but who are you two?"

"I'm Sylvia Burns," the woman with the silver bun said.

"I'm Helga Wells," the red-haired woman said. "I'm Gary's grandmother's sister."

"And you all three live here?" McNulty asked.

"Yes," Sylvia said. "And we've all been ogled by that goggle-wearing perv!"

"The man was a menace," Geraldine said. "We kept changing the times we'd do our water aerobics, but it didn't help. The creep's trailer is that green one right over there. It overlooks the pool. Any time he'd spot us he'd come running over to do his peeping-frog act."

My nose crinkled. "Couldn't you do anything else to stop him? Like, an ordinance or something?"

"We tried," Helga said. "But there were no HOA regulations against it. Everyone is free to use the pool between the hours of dawn and dusk."

"Besides, you can't regulate crazy," Sylvia said. "Who knew we'd have to deal with some perv wearing goggles?"

I grimaced. "Couldn't you vote him out of the community?"

Sylvia shook her head. "Unfortunately, no."

My brow furrowed. "Why not?"

Geraldine blew out a sigh. "It's the age-old story, Fremden. Orville was loaded. We had to put up with his crap because we needed his money."

My nose crinkled. "You mean for the fair?"

"Yeah," Sylvia said. "Among other things. Like when the pool heater broke this past winter. Orville ponied up the money to get it fixed."

"Wow," I said. "*That* wasn't self-serving at all."

"Last time Orville came to the pool in goggles, I told him to get lost," Helga said. "We all got out and left."

"The next day he cancelled his sponsorship of the fair," Geraldine said. "That's why I was so crabby when you and I had lunch."

Is that also why you were carrying a gun?

"Enough with the questions, Fremden," McNulty said, coming back from positioning another officer at the pool gate with a notepad. "I'm leading this investigation, not you." He studied the four of us for a moment. "From what I overheard, Ledbetter was a man of means. But then his generosity dried up."

"Yeah," Geraldine said. "So?"

"So," McNulty said, "when Ledbetter wouldn't foot the bills anymore, there was no longer any reason to put up with his behavior, *or to keep him alive.*"

The three older women shared furtive glances amongst themselves but said nothing. It was McNulty who broke the silence.

"Did any of you witness anyone arguing with Ledbetter recently? Or know of anyone who might've held a grudge against him?"

"Besides us?" Geraldine asked. "Yeah. Pretty much everybody who knew him."

Chapter Seventeen

As I snarfed down the last bite of a maple-glazed donut, out of the corner of my eye I caught sight of an EMT coming through the guarded pool gate. He was being led in by the young cop I knew as Officer Brady.

McNulty saw the EMT arrive, too. "I need you all to remain here for individual questioning," he said to the crowd lingering around the pool area. "I mean you, too, Fremden. What do you know about all this?"

I nearly choked. "Um ... next to nothing, sir!"

His eyes narrowed as he pulled me aside. "You and Jiggles are business partners now. Has she ever mentioned Orville Ledbetter to you?"

"Um ... only a couple of days ago. She told me he dropped out of sponsoring the fair. She was pretty mad about it. But then she cooled down when I offered to cover expenses so the fair could go on."

McNulty's left eyebrow rose an inch. "*You* covered expenses? How much?"

"Um ... $4,500."

"That's a lot of cash. Where'd you get it?"

I winced. "I don't *have* to tell you ... do I?"

McNulty's eyes narrowed even further. His head slanted slightly. "Why wouldn't you want to tell me?"

I blew out a breath. "It was a business loan, okay?"

To my amazement, McNulty blanched. "A *bank* loaned you money?"

I jutted my chin up an inch higher. "No. My best friend did, okay?"

"What'd you do? Hold a gun to her head?"

It was my turn to blanch. "What? No!" My hackles rose with Southern indignation. "Unlike Geraldine, I don't even *own* a gun, much less carry one around in my purse."

McNulty's eyebrows collided. "Jiggles carries a gun in her purse? How do you know that?"

"Uh ... we went to lunch together the other day and she ... she pulled it out."

"In a restaurant?" McNulty whipped off his mirrored sunglasses and studied my face like there might be a test about it later. "Why? Did she threaten you with it?"

"No! I mean ... at first, I thought she was. But then I realized it wasn't like that. She told me she was practicing for the shootout with it. Honestly, I don't think Geraldine even remembered she had the gun in her purse."

"What type of gun was it?"

"The same one she just used in the shootout. A Junior Commando." I stared at McNulty's shoes, feeling like a narc. "Look. Geraldine is an ornery old cuss, sure. But I don't think she'd actually *kill* anybody. At least, not intentionally."

I glanced up at him. McNulty's eagle eyes bored into mine. "This is serious," he said. "A man is dead. If you have any pertinent information, you'd better tell me. *Now.*"

I glanced around the crowd. No one appeared to be listening in. "I don't know if this is pertinent or not, but a couple of days ago I overheard some women at the clubhouse discussing 'taking care of a pervert.' At the time, I'd assumed they'd meant Rooster. The mower."

McNulty crossed his arms. "A perverted lawn mower? Now I've heard everything, Fremden."

I fidgeted on my feet. "Not the *machine*. The *guy mowing*. His name is Carl something or other. I saw him mowing the clubhouse grounds this morning. He must've headed over to the shootout right after I did. He was the fourth shooter. Randy Dandy."

"Enough with all these stupid nicknames," McNulty said. He put his sunglasses back on and took a step toward the EMTs. Then he stopped, lowered his glasses, and peered at me over them. "Wait a minute. Where were you when you saw Randy ... Rooster ... ugh! The *fourth shooter*?"

"I was here ... at the pool—"

"You were at the pool this morning?"

My gut flopped with a familiar feeling. How was it that McNulty could make me feel guilty even when I was innocent?

"Um ... yes, sir," I said. "I helped Winky set up all of these floats and the donuts at the tiki hut. You remember Winky? He was Dough Nut, the second shoot—"

"I remember him," McNulty said. "Was he with you the whole time?"

"Yes!" I practically squealed, relieved I had a ready alibi. But then I remembered I kind of didn't. "Well, no, sir. Not the whole time. Winky left a little early to sign some papers for Geraldine."

I could feel McNulty's eyes boring into me through his mirrored lenses. "How much earlier?" he demanded.

I withered a little. "I dunno exactly. Maybe twenty minutes?"

McNulty smiled the kind of smile that had nothing to do with happiness. "In other words," he said, "you were alone at the pool with plenty of time to shoot a man and cover him up with donut floats."

Chapter Eighteen

"**I** didn't do it!" I yelped. I glanced around the pool area, desperate for some way to convince McNulty I didn't kill Orville Ledbetter. "Wait. I know! Saurwein can vouch for me!"

I spotted the wisecracking reporter over by the tiki hut, stuffing a donut into her mouth. I sprinted over to her. Without a word, I yanked her by the arm across the pool deck and shoved her in front of McNulty. I could tell by the hardened look on his face that my plan had better work.

"Tell him," I demanded.

Saurwein jerked her arm free. "Tell who what?"

"Tell Officer McNulty you were with me when I left the pool this morning," I said. "You know, to go to the shootout. Tell him there wasn't a body floating in the pool when I left!"

Saurwein looked me up and down and smirked. She smiled sweetly up at McNulty. "Sorry, officer. I met Fremden *outside* the pool gate. I never looked at the pool itself."

"What?" I gasped. "Come on!"

"Hold on," McNulty said. "Was Fremden acting strangely?"

Saurwein laughed. "When is she *not*?"

"Did she appear nervous," McNulty asked. "Jittery. In over her head?"

Saurwein smirked. "Like I said, when is she *not*?"

"Thanks a lot," I hissed at Saurwein. "Look, Officer McNulty. I had nothing to do with this. I don't even own a gun! Test my hands for gunpowder. I insist!"

"Brady!" McNulty called out to the young cop. Brady was busy shooing oglers away while the EMTs hauled Ledbetter's body out of the pool.

"Yes, sir!" Brady said, sprinting up to us with a clipboard. "I've collected the names and numbers of the people in the pool area. Should I release them now?"

"Not yet," McNulty said. "Round up the shooters and send them into the clubhouse. I'll do the interviews inside."

"The shooters, sir?" Brady asked. "You know who did this?"

"I meant the fair's shootout contestants," McNulty said. "There are four of them." He turned to me. "What are their names?"

I gulped. "Um ... Captain Commando, Silver—"

"I meant their *real* names!" McNulty growled.

"Oh." I thought for a second. "Geraldine, Winky, Sylvia with the silver bun, and the mower guy ... you know, Carl something or other."

"Ugh," McNulty groaned. "Can you pick them out of this crowd?"

I nodded. "Yes, sir."

"Then go with Brady and find them," McNulty said.

"I can pick them out, too," Saurwein said.

McNulty eyed her with suspicion. "On second thought, both of you come with me. Brady, I want you to locate a GSR test kit and wipe down Fremden's hands for gunpowder residue ASAP."

"Yes, sir," Brady said. "I'm on it!"

• • • •

SEATED AT A CHEAP FOLDING table, I watched Saurwein watching me from across the clubhouse as I got swabbed down by Officer Brady. While I was holding my breath for the results, she was holding interviews with the shootout contestants—namely Winky, Geraldine and Sylvia.

"The GSR is negative," Brady said finally. "She's clean. No gunpowder."

I shot an indignant frown at McNulty, who was sitting across the table from me. "I told you. I didn't even *know* the victim. Why would I want to shoot him?"

McNulty pursed his lips. "It's standard procedure, Fremden. We're eliminating suspects one by one."

I nearly fell off my chair, knocked over by a giant wave of relief. "Does that mean I'm cleared? I'm free to go?"

"Yes. For now." McNulty glanced around the clubhouse.

I bolted up from my chair.

"Not so fast," McNulty said. "You appear to know your way around this place. I'd appreciate your cooperation in helping us navigate this crowd to determine who might be a potential suspect."

"But sir, I don't know anybody—"

"Look at them all out there." McNulty nodded toward the sliding glass windows. Outside, a horde of people were milling around the pool. "I need to interview everyone Brady sends this way. After I talk with the shootout contestants, I want to start with the women you told me about earlier."

"What women?" I asked.

"The ones you said you saw here at the clubhouse a few days ago. The ones you said you overheard talking about getting rid of a pervert."

My nose crinkled. "Oh. You think Orville Ledbetter could be the pervert they meant?"

McNulty's eyes narrowed. "I'd bet on it."

"I thought everyone was innocent until proven guilty."

McNulty crossed his arms. "They are—until they're caught in a public pool wearing a speedo and goggles. I mean, how many other perverts could these women have been talking about?"

I sighed. "I keep forgetting you just moved here from Vegas."

McNulty scowled. "Fremden, just go tell Geraldine Jiggles to come over to me. Then you and Saurwein round up the other women that were in the clubhouse the other day. Do you know who they are?"

"Most of them, sir. They were Geraldine, Sylvia, Helga, and some lady with a Jersey accent."

"Jersey accent? She shouldn't be too hard to pick out."

I shook my head. "You really are a Florida newbie, aren't you?"

"Can it," McNulty said. "Now, get Saurwein and find those missing women."

"Yes, sir."

"Oh," McNulty called out as I turned to go. "Also find the other male shootout contestant. What was his name?"

"Randy Dandy?" I said.

McNulty scowled. "I meant his *real* name."

My nose crinkled. "Rooster?"

McNulty shook his head. "Geez. Why did I transfer to Florida? *Why*?"

Chapter Nineteen

As I walked across the clubhouse to fetch Geraldine for Officer McNulty, I realized she was no longer at the table with Saurwein and Sylvia. Neither was Winky.

"Where'd Geraldine go?" I asked.

"I was done with her," Saurwein said. "She went out to the pool."

"What about Winky?"

Saurwein frowned. "He went to the restroom and never came back."

Thankfully, it didn't take long to locate either one of them.

As soon as I stepped out of the clubhouse, I spotted Geraldine over at the pool's tiki cabana. She and two other women I'd spied on at the clubhouse earlier in the week had commandeered the coffee and donut station. Like a trio of lunch ladies on crack, they were frantically stuffing Winky's free donuts into gallon-sized plastic baggies.

"What are you doing?" I asked, startling the Jersey lady.

"What's it look like we're doing?" she snarled. "Shining shoes?"

"Geez, Fremden," Geraldine said as she crammed a baggie stuffed with crullers into her oversized purse. "What part of *Survivalist Fair* do you not understand?"

"Watch out, Val-Pal!" Winky hollered, peeking around the side of the tiki hut. "Don't get near 'em. You could lose a finger!"

I felt for him. The way those women were heisting Winky's donuts, I wouldn't have been surprised if they were planning to hogtie him and hold him for ransom.

"Enough with the donut heist, ladies!" I shouted. "I need you all to come with me. You, too, Winky. Sergeant McNulty wants to talk to each of you."

"Coppers," the Jersey woman said. "They're always spoiling the fun."

"Come on, follow me," I said, then grabbed one of the remaining donuts for my own survival. I herded Winky and the women into the clubhouse. McNulty sat waiting impatiently at the head of a small folding table, a notepad in his hand.

"Change of plans," McNulty said as I approached. "I'll start with your pal Winky."

"Good idea," I said. "That way Winky can get back to defending his donut stand."

"Defending his donut stand?" McNulty asked.

"You should see them people, Sarge," Winky said, wringing his hands. "It's like Custard's Last Stand out there!"

"Ugh," McNulty groaned. "Enough with the lame jokes already."

"Who's jokin'?" Winky asked, his eyes darting from McNulty to me and back again.

McNulty sighed. "Just hand me your I.D. and take a seat."

Winky nodded. "You got it, Chief."

McNulty turned his attention to me. "Fremden, I want you to keep an eye on the others. Don't let them wander off again."

"Yes, sir."

"And make sure my recorder is working at all times." McNulty motioned for me to join him and Winky at the table, then shoved a small tape recorder at me.

"Yes, sir." Uncertain as to how I was supposed to accomplish both tasks at the same time, I slunk into the chair across the table from Winky.

My freckled friend pulled his driver's license from his wallet and slid it across the table. "Here you go, sir."

"Wallace Winchell," McNulty said, taking the ID and reading it aloud. "You were with Val Fremden at the pool this morning, correct?"

"Yessir."

"Did you see anything suspicious?"

"No sir. And there weren't nobody dead when I left for the shootout. I can guarantee it. I was the one throwin' donuts in the pool. The floatin' kind, I mean."

"Noted," McNulty said. "What type of gun did you bring for the shootout?"

"Nary a one. On account a I wasn't plannin' on being in the shootout. Geraldine asked me to, 'cause somebody dropped out. It was a last-minute thang, you see."

McNulty handed Winky back his I.D. "So, where'd you get the gun?"

Winky slipped the license back into his wallet. "It was Davy Eber what lent me the gun. An old timey one. A dad-burned Ruger Bearcat Revolver with a wooden grip. I've always wanted to shoot me one!"

McNulty's brow furrowed. "Are you saying you won the shootout competition with a gun you'd never fired before?"

Winky grinned with pride. "Yeppers. And now I get to eat all the sushi I want."

"How do you account for that?"

"With this here coupon!" Winky whipped the Poke Bowl coupon from his front pocket.

McNulty let out a small groan. "No. I meant how do you account for your excellent aim?"

"Oh." Winky leaned back in the chair and cupped his hands behind his head. "I get me lots a practice. Mostly with my old Mossberg shotgun. I shoot at critters back home all the time. In fact, folks around my 'hood call me 'Ol' One-Shot.'"

"Old One-Shot?" McNulty asked.

"Yep. On account I can pick off a squirrel at a hundred yards with one shot."

McNulty leaned in closer to Winky. "That's a pretty small target. What part of the animal do you aim for?"

"The cranium," Winky said. "Right between their beady little eyes."

The corners of McNulty's mouth curled slightly. "You don't say."

"No sir," Winky said. "I mean yessir, I *do* say."

I cringed, hoping McNulty realized Winky was way too naïve to be a good liar, much less a killer.

"All right," McNulty said. "That's it for now, Mr. Winchell. You're free to go defend your donuts, for now."

"Thank you, Sarge. I sure hope you catch the rascal what shot Mr. Goggles." Winky got up, saluted us both, and left.

McNulty turned to me. "Fremden, I want to talk to this Randy Dandy Rooster guy next."

"Um ... I'm sorry," I said. "Everyone else was at the tiki hut, so I herded them inside while I had the chance. I didn't see Rooster out there."

McNulty bolted up out of his chair and yelled, "Winchell!"

Winky froze in place at the threshold of the clubhouse's sliding glass doors, one foot in and one out. He put his hands in the air and slowly turned around. I'd never seen his eyes so huge. "Am I under arrest?" he asked.

"No!" McNulty said. "I want you to find this Rooster fellow. Think you can do that for me?"

Winky nodded. "Sure thang, Sarge." Poor Winky took a longing glance at the tiki hut. "Looks like they done cleaned out my donut stand anyways."

"Too bad. Now get going!" McNulty said, then turned and glared at me. "Who's the other shooter?"

"Silver Bun ... I mean Silver Hammer ... I mean Sylvia," I said. I motioned toward the lady with the silver bun. As she walked over to us, I filled in McNulty. "FYI, she participated in the shootout *and* she was one of the women I overheard talking about 'getting rid of the pervert,' sir."

Sylvia crinkled her nose at me. "Snitches get stitches, you know."

"Have a seat and give me your I.D. please," McNulty said.

"Whatever you say, Mr. Policeman," she said.

McNulty shook his head tiredly, then took the ID and studied it briefly. "Sylvia Burns. Can you tell me who you were referring to earlier in the week when you and your clubhouse friends discussed 'getting rid of a pervert'?"

Burns tightened her grip on the giant purse in her lap. "Well ... yes. We were talking about Carl Menendez."

"Not Orville Ledbetter?" McNulty asked.

"Well, no, not on that particular occasion," Burns said.

"Just exactly how many perverts are running around your trailer park?" McNulty asked, then glanced over at me. "Never mind. Florida."

"Carl Menendez is Rooster, aka Randy Dandy," I said to McNulty. "So I was right all along."

"We're not keeping score here, Fremden," McNulty said. "And enough with all these nicknames already! Ms. Burns. Do you know the current whereabouts of Carl Menendez?"

Burns shook her head. "No. All I can say is, unlike Orville, Rooster was never around when you wanted him."

McNulty cocked his head. "What do you mean by that?"

Burns sniffed. "Nothing."

McNulty scowled. "What type of weapon did you fire in the shootout?"

Burns' face brightened. "A .22 Ruger Mark IV."

McNulty's left eyebrow rose a notch. "That's some serious hardware."

Burns shrugged. "Florida is a serious place to live."

"I'm finding that out," McNulty said. "Do you know what type of weapon Menendez used in the competition?"

"Um ... no."

"You were standing right beside him."

Burns blushed. "I wasn't looking at his *gun*."

McNulty sighed again. "Ms. Burns. Did you shoot Orville Ledbetter?"

The old woman gasped. "What? No! I fired three rounds during the competition and that's it! You can check the chamber." She reached into her humongous purse and pulled out a gallon-sized baggie crammed with donuts. She set them on the table, then fished out the Ruger, her finger on the trigger.

"Whoa!" McNulty said, bolting back in his chair. "Put the gun down on the table. *Gently*."

"What else would I do with it?" Burns said, laying the gun down.

McNulty reached over and pushed the barrel of the gun with his pen until it was no longer aimed at anyone. "Ms. Burns, do you know anyone who would want to harm Orville Ledbetter?"

"Well, sure," she said, smiling up at McNulty. "Geraldine. After all, *she* was the one going out with him."

Chapter Twenty

"Geraldine was going out with Orville?" I gasped at the revelation freshly spewed from the mouth of Sylvia Burns. My eyes darted to the folding table where Geraldine had been sitting with the two other women waiting to be interviewed. She was gone. *Again.* "What the—"

"Thanks for ratting me out, Sylvia," Geraldine's gravelly voice sounded right behind me. I turned to see Geraldine standing near the table, holding up her hands. "Guilty as charged, Officer McNulty."

"Told you," Burns said, sneering at Geraldine.

"Goggles?" I asked. "How could you?"

"You've gotta understand," Geraldine said. "Dating at my age is like shopping at my thrift store. The best you can do is find something with the least wear and tear and fewest missing pieces."

"Sure," Burns said, shooting eye daggers at Geraldine. "I'm sure that the fact Orville was loaded had nothing to do with it."

McNulty cleared his throat loudly. Everyone shut up. Like a game of Spin the Bottle, we all waited to see where his laser focus would land next. It was Geraldine. "I'm going to need to see your ID," he said. "And your gun."

"My gun?" Geraldine asked. "Why?"

"I'm collecting all the weapons used in the shootout. For ballistics testing. I'll need yours, too, Ms. Burns."

"Testing?" Burns asked, clutching her purse a little tighter.

"Yes," McNulty said. "For comparison against the bullet in Ledbetter's head."

"Geez Louise," Geraldine said. She reached into her purse and fished out the dull-silver handgun. She laid it on the table next to Burns's Ruger Mark IV.

McNulty pulled on a pair of rubber gloves and put both Geraldine's and Burns's guns into separate evidence bags. "You'll get these back when the case is solved," he said.

"We'd better," Geraldine said.

McNulty's right eyebrow rose a notch. "I'm curious. How did Orville Ledbetter get his money?"

"He owned Looker's Eyewear," Burns said, shooting Geraldine a *put that in your pipe and smoke it* look.

"Looker's Eyewear?" I frowned. "Saurwein told me she dropped an ad for that place in the *Beach Gazette* so she could put in ours."

"That sounds like quite the favor," McNulty said. "Why would she do that for you, Fremden? I thought you two hated each other."

I chewed my bottom lip. "She owed me a favor. Saurwein said it wasn't that big a deal anyway. She told me she didn't expect the old geezer would be in any condition to complain about it."

"Did she now?" McNulty said, his left eyebrow an inch higher than his right. "I wonder what she meant by that."

"I don't know, sir." At the other end of the clubhouse, Saurwein was sitting at a table interviewing Gary Wells, the balloon guy whose main act had ended up in a spectacular bellyflop. From the look on his face, he needed rescuing yet again.

I hopped up out of my chair. "Let me get her and you can ask her yourself."

• • • •

"THE DEAD GUY IN THE pool is the owner of Looker's Eyewear?" Saurwein asked, sliding into the seat previously occupied by Burns. "I had no idea!"

McNulty wasn't having it. "Really? Then why did you tell Fremden he wasn't in any condition to complain about his ad being replaced with hers?"

"Because he's old as dirt," Saurwein said.

McNulty scoffed. "That's hardly a reason for—"

"Okay, Okay," Saurwein said. "When I was at his shop taking photos for his ad, the letch pinched my butt."

McNulty sighed. "Apparently this guy really got around. When did this happen?"

"Last week," Saurwein said. "I told the creep if he touched me again, I'd call the cops."

"Or maybe shoot him?" I quipped.

Saurwein glared at me. "Hey, I wasn't the one walking around with a bullet hole in the back of my shirt."

"What?" McNulty asked, his raven eyes landing dead on mine.

"It was nothing, sir!" I blurted. "It was just some dumb shirt I'd found."

"Found where?" McNulty asked.

I grimaced and glanced over at Geraldine, still perched in a chair at the table. "Um ... in a bin at Belated Rooms."

Saurwein smirked. "Poor Geraldine. Looks like all roads keep leading back to you."

"That's what she gets for 'Rome'-ing the neighborhood for Romeos," a woman's Jersey voice sounded behind me.

I turned around to see the smug, tobacco-tanned face of a woman with hair as white as a cotton ball. She was the fourth woman who'd been at the clubhouse the day Winky and I'd been busted during our stupid stakeout attempt.

"Who are you?" McNulty asked.

"Name's Lucille Murman," she said, shooting Geraldine and Sylvia Burns a flippant glance. "But unlike those two ladies, I don't need a gun to get a date."

Chapter Twenty-One

"Here's my ID," the well-dressed woman said. She handed McNulty her driver's license, sending a cadre of silver bangles tumbling down her tanned forearm to her wrist.

"Lucille Murman," McNulty said, studying the cotton-haired woman's license. "When did you last see Orville Ledbetter?"

"Alive? Around noon," Murman said with a shrug. "I stopped by the pool for a quick dip, but when I saw all those donut floats I decided to sunbathe instead. Then—"

"That was after I left!" I blurted, poking McNulty on the shoulder. "That proves Ledbetter was still alive after I left!"

"Got it," McNulty said, shooting me an annoyed glare. "Please continue, Ms. Murman."

"Well, I was about to take off my Talbot's beach wrap when I spotted Orville—or should I say *he* spotted *me*. The jerk came flying out of his filthy trailer in that damned speedo. I decided to grab my stuff up and get out of there."

"Where was Ledbetter when you left?" McNulty asked.

"Putting his goggles on and wading into the pool at the steps," Murman said, shooting a knowing glance at the other ladies. "Of course, he didn't shower first."

"Of course not," Burns said. "Pig."

"Was anyone else in the pool area?" McNulty asked.

"No," Murman said. "But as I left, Rooster rode by on his mower. He was just finishing the last strip of lawn. I waved him down, but he said he couldn't stop. He was heading to the shootout. I watched him ride his mower up the ramp into his utility cart, then take off running in the direction of the shootout."

"Interesting. During any of this, did you hear a gunshot?" McNulty asked.

"No."

"Thank you, Ms. Murman. Just one more question. Do you own a gun?"

She smirked. "No. Like I said, I don't need one."

• • • •

I WAS ABOUT TO PUT out an APB on Winky when he finally returned to the clubhouse. Tasked by McNulty to find Rooster, the elusive mowing man was still at large. But my friend didn't come back empty handed.

"Sorry, Sarge," Winky said, shuffling up to the table where I sat along with McNulty and Geraldine. "I couldn't find Rooster, but I found somebody I thought could help. This antique guy right here."

"Hey, I'm not *that* old," Davy Eber said with a wink. "What can I do for you, Officer McNulty?"

"We can't locate Rooster—Carl Menendez," McNulty said. "Do you know what type of weapon he used in the shootout competition?"

"I sure do," Eber said. "A .38 Special."

"A .38," McNulty repeated. "And what was the weapon you lent to Mr. Winchell?"

Eber appeared confused. Winky elbowed him. "He means me."

"Oh," Eber said. "A Ruger Bearcat Revolver."

McNulty nodded. "What type of ammo does it use?"

"It shoots .22s," Eber said. "Why?"

"We're going to need it for ballistics comparisons," McNulty said.

"Sure thing," Eber said. "I'll go get it."

"I'd appreciate that," McNulty said. "But one more thing before you do."

"What's that?" Eber asked.

"I'm going to need you to get that microphone of yours and make an announcement." McNulty glanced around the clubhouse. "As of now, the entire fairgrounds are considered a crime scene. I want you to inform the public that the fair's cancelled and they need to clear out."

"What?" Geraldine gasped. "Blast that stupid Orville, how am I supposed to make my money back now?"

Eber shook his head and glared at Geraldine. "You know, maybe you should've thought about that before you did him in!"

"Did him in?" McNulty asked. "What are you talking about, Eber?"

Eber hung his head. "I didn't put two and two together until now. Yesterday morning when I walked into Belated Rooms I overheard Val talking with Geraldine. She said something to the effect of, 'Don't worry about it Geraldine. I've got Goggles taken care of.'"

Chapter Twenty-Two

McNulty stared at me. "And I was just beginning to believe you had nothing to do with Orville Ledbetter's death. Care to explain yourself?"

I wracked my brain, trying to figure out what Eber was talking about when he said he'd heard me talking about 'taking care of Goggles.' Then it hit me. "I got it! When Eber came into the shop yesterday, I *was* talking about goggles. But not the perver—*man*, the *eyewear.* I need protective goggles for my new shop, Simply Smashing."

"She's telling the truth," Geraldine said. "When Davy came in, we were going over the list so we wouldn't get sued. Our liability coverage requires Fremden to supply customers with overalls, helmets, hammers, gloves, and gog—"

"Simply Smashing?" McNulty asked. "What kind of store requires customers to dress like they're going into battle?"

"Mine," I said. "You see, Simply Smashing lets people take a hammer and ... uh ... smash things to bits."

McNulty shook his head. "Well, I have to hand it to you, Fremden. You've found a way to maximize your potential." He glanced around at all of us like a man trapped in a never-ending freakshow. "You're all free to go for now," he said, grabbing up the guns he'd collected for evidence. "But don't leave town."

"What about the fair?" I asked.

"Right." McNulty turned to Eber. "Get that mic of yours and start announcing to the crowd that the fair is cancelled, effective immediately. I'll inform my officers to make sure everyone leaves in an orderly fashion."

"But—" Geraldine objected.

But it was no use. Before she could get another word in edgewise, Officer McNulty turned and marched right out the clubhouse's sliding glass doors.

• • • •

"WOO, DOGGY," WINKY said, shaking his head as we slunk out of the clubhouse following McNulty's unexpected announcement.

"I can't believe he cancelled the fair," Geraldine grumbled. She was mad as a hornet as we watched disgruntled fairgoers head for their cars and peel out of the parking lot. She shook her head. "This is a disaster."

"You ain't kiddin'," Winky said. "I ain't seen this many ruffled feathers since Aunt Vera shot a goose-down pillow thinkin' it was the ghost a Uncle Cletus come back to haunt her."

"Maybe it's for the best," I said. "Goggles floating dead in the pool put a damper on things. But the way you ladies were talking smack to each other in the clubhouse, it seemed like an encore performance wasn't out of the question."

"She's right," Winky said. "Aunt Vera always said, 'Criticism ain't a gift of the Holy Spirit.'"

"Eh," Geraldine scowled, picking a stone out of her green croc. "Those old broads are just jealous."

"Jealous of what?" I asked.

"Helga got a DUI, lost her license, and can't drive anymore," Geraldine said. "She's always chasing us on that bicycle of hers. As for Sylvia, she thinks I stole her man."

"That Orville fella?" Winky asked.

Geraldine sneered. "Yeah. She thinks she's so hot to trot. But the tramp got kicked out of The Villages, for crying out loud."

My nose crinkled. "Isn't that place the STD capital of Florida?"

"Yeah." Geraldine shook a finger at me. "But what they don't tell you is that the S stands for Sylvia."

Winky hooted with laughter. "What about Lucille?" he asked, digging for dirt. "What's *she* so mad at you about?"

"Jersey Girl just opened her own thrift shop down the road from here. Lucille's Lucky Finds. She blames me for not being able to find good merch for her shop."

"Why would she blame you for that?" I asked.

Geraldine shrugged. "Blame is like a crow, Fremden. It always seems to find a place to land."

"Speakin' of comin' home to roost," Winky said. "Don't y'all find it kinda strange ol' Rooster ain't nowhere to be found?"

Geraldine smirked. "Knowing him, he's busy doing undercover work."

"He's a detective?" Winky asked.

"More like a dog," Geraldine said. "One that can sniff out a woman in heat."

Winky smiled good-naturedly. "Well, it sure can get hot around here, that's for sure."

Geraldine shot me a *seriously?* expression.

"Oh, look at that," I said. "We're at the van."

"You need a ride home, Ms. G?" Winky asked, opening the driver's door.

"Yeah, Geraldine," I said. "It's no problem."

Geraldine shook her head. "I *live* here, geniuses."

"Oh, right," I said. "My condolences."

• • • •

ON THE DRIVE HOME FROM the clubhouse, I nearly sweated through my clothes from the heat.

"Sorry, Val-Pal, the AC's on the fritz," Winky said. "If'n we could find Rooster, maybe he could help you with the heat. You know, like Geraldine said."

"I'll pass." I wiped the sweat from my brow with a paper napkin I swiped from the glovebox. "Ugh! I don't know what people did before air conditioning."

Winky cocked his head and looked at me sideways. "They sweated."

"I know. I just meant ... wait a minute. Did you notice how sweaty Geraldine was when she came running out of the ladies' room this morning?"

Winky kept his eyes on the road. "My mama taught me not to mention nothin' about a person doin' their natural-born doody. That and the heartbreak of psoriasis."

"I'm serious, Winky. At the clubhouse this morning when Geraldine came out and asked us to help her fix the toilet. She looked sweaty. That woman *never* sweats!"

"Like my mama said, a person's toilet habits is their own business."

"Winky, you said the problem was a loose tube in the toilet tank. What could cause that to happen?"

Winky shrugged. "I dunno. Wear and tear?"

"Could it have gotten bumped or pulled loose?"

"I guess so. But by who?" Winky laughed. "Only person I know what's swimmin' inside a toilet tank is the Ty-D-Bol man."

I frowned. "What if someone *hid* something in there? Like a gun?"

"But there weren't no gun in there," Winky said.

"No, because Geraldine had already taken it out. That's why her arms looked sweaty. It was toilet-tank water!"

Winky hit the brakes. His eyes grew as big as boiled eggs. "Are you sayin' Geraldine shot Orville?"

I cringed. "I don't know. When it comes to money, I'm not sure there's anything she's not capable of doing."

Winky nodded thoughtfully. "And from what I heard, this here Orville fella had plenty a dough to squeeze out."

"He did." I swallowed hard. "There's more. When I went into the shop yesterday morning, I heard Geraldine on the phone talking to someone about getting rid of something."

Winky tapped a pudgy finger on his freckled noggin. "Sure it wasn't some*one*?"

I grimaced and shook my head. "It couldn't be. She wouldn't, would she?"

"Well, you know, I wasn't gonna say nothin'," Winky said. "But when I was settin' up your shop, I got a good look at that stuff you bought off a Rooster. I'd say a goodly portion of it had bullet holes in it."

My mouth fell open. "Geraldine told me she'd been practicing for the shootout. Do you think that—"

"Maybe she got a little carried away?" Winky pursed his lips. "I guess we'll have to wait and see what the powers that be have to say about that."

Powers that be?

The words sparked a memory. "Winky, remember what Rooster said the day we bought the junk from him? He said he had some kind of arrangement with the 'powers that be' about collecting the junk from the side of the road."

"Yep, I do recall that."

"Who do you think that arrangement was with?"

"Prolly somebody who wanted the stuff for themselves."

"Of course! It would have to be Lucille or Geraldine. They both have junk shops."

"Maybe both." Winky poked me on the shoulder. "Don't forget, now *you're* on that list, too, Val-Pal."

"You're right!" I cringed. "They're junk rivals. Do you think they may have been rivals for Orville, too?"

"Cain't rightly say. All we know for sure is *somebody* got rid of Orville. And now maybe Rooster as well."

I gasped. "You think he's been murdered, too?"

"Either that or he's undercover somewhere workin' on some poor woman's heat."

I shook my head.

Oh, lord. I need to get out of here. He's starting to make sense.

I was relieved that we were almost to my house. "Winky, it sounded to me like there was a lot of weird stuff going on at that trailer park."

"Sure was," Winky said, pulling up to my driveway. "And there's only one thing we can do about it."

"What?" I asked, popping open the van door.

"Have us another stakeout, a course!"

I nodded. "I'll think about it. Thanks for driving."

"Anytime, Val-Pal!"

I climbed out of the van and headed to my door. For once, I wasn't on the hook with McNulty. He'd pretty much cleared me already. But after seeing Lucille, Helga, Sylvia, and Geraldine competing with each other over the shrinking supply of men in their dried-up dating pool, I had the sinking feeling one of them had killed Orville Ledbetter—either because they *didn't* have him, or they *did*.

If I was right, there was a one-in-four chance Geraldine did it. And given what I knew about her hot temper, I didn't like the odds.

Chapter Twenty-Three

"How was the fair?" Tom asked as I came through the door feeling bewildered about Geraldine's one-in-four chance of being Orville Ledbetter's killer.

"Not great," I said, tossing my purse onto the coffee table. "McNulty shut it down. Tomorrow's events are all cancelled."

"I heard over the police radio." Tom winced sympathetically. "Dead guy in the pool, huh?"

"Yeah."

Tom hugged me. "I'm sorry. I'm sure the community was just as disappointed as you."

I sighed and flopped onto the couch. "I doubt it."

"What do you mean?"

"I need a drink first."

Tom laughed. "Coming right up."

As Tom padded to the kitchen, I realized I couldn't exactly share my fears with him about Geraldine being the world's oldest murderer. Besides, there were plenty of other reasons for me to be upset.

I could count 4,500 of them right off the bat.

"The fair was supposed to put Geraldine's and my store on the map," I called out as Tom scooped ice from the freezer into a cocktail glass.

"Well, it did. Today," Tom said.

"Not nearly enough." I picked at the fringe on a throw pillow. "Like a stupid jerk I invested all of my start-up money into it."

"Oh. Well, at least you got *today's* earnings back," Tom said, pouring gin into the ice.

"That's just it." I tossed the pillow aside. "Tomorrow was supposed to be our big moneymaker. Sunday's cakewalk, dunking booths, and carnival games were going to help us recoup our entire investment."

Tom handed me the Tanqueray and tonic. "Cheer up," he said, picking up the TV remote and clicking the set on. "Maybe you'll get a refund?"

"From those skinflints at the trailer park? I doubt it." I took a sip of my cocktail and sighed. "What have I done, Tom? The money I borrowed from Milly is gone. Now our businesses are on borrowed time. How could this get any worse?"

Then, as if to prove a point, it did.

A familiar voice was emanating from the TV. "Holy crap!" I said. "Tom, look!" Shirley Saurwein's smug face was mugging for the camera, taking up the full TV screen. "Turn up the volume!"

Tom clicked the remote, then sat down on the couch beside me.

"On my latest installment of 'This Could Only Happen in Florida,' the Queen of the Road Survivalist Fair was supposed to make a big splash with the community today," Saurwein said. In the background, a clip of Gary Wells crash-landing his balloon chair in the clubhouse pool played over and over.

I groaned and took another swig of my gin and tonic.

Saurwein droned on: "But the fair's kick-off event led to someone else kicking off in an entirely different way."

Suddenly, a video of Orville Ledbetter being pulled from the pool began to play, while an image of his face flashed onto the corner of the screen.

"Last year's event sponsor, Orville Ledbetter, was found floating in the trailer park's community pool with a bullet between his eyes," Saurwein said with a gleam in hers. "Yes, folks, it looks like Led*better*'s seen *better* days."

Tom groaned. "As far as shots go, they don't get much cheaper."

"Hush!" I said, slapping him gently on the knee. "I want to hear this!"

"As of this moment," Saurwein continued, "this year's Queen of the Road Survivalist Fair has been cancelled by the St. Petersburg Police Department. A murder investigation is underway."

Saurwein shoved her microphone into the face of a perturbed looking policeman. "Sergeant McNulty, do you have any suspects in the murder?"

"I can't discuss an open investigation," McNulty said through gritted teeth. "But we are actively pursuing leads."

"Would those leads include the new fair sponsors?" Saurwein asked.

"The nerve!" I hissed.

McNulty scowled. "At this point, we aren't ruling out anyone with ties to the victim."

Saurwein grinned like the Grinch who stole Neilsen ratings, then turned to face the audience. "There you have it, folks. It appears that *fair* play has turned to *foul* play in St. Petersburg. But rest assured, it's just a matter of time before the guilty hens come home to roost."

"Ugh," I groaned and clicked off the TV.

"Guilty hens?" Tom asked.

"Most of the seniors McNulty interviewed about the crime were elderly female residents," I said. "Forget her. Saurwein's imagination is even stupider than her puns."

Tom studied me for a moment. "Then why do you look so worried? Is there something you're not telling me? McNulty hasn't tried to put any of this on *you* again, I hope."

"No. I mean, he tried, but I had an alibi. It's not me I'm worried about. It's Geraldine. I'm afraid he might have his eye on her for the crime."

Tom set his beer on the coffee table and took my hand. "Why do you think that?"

I shrugged and stared at the condensation trickling down his beer bottle. "Just a feeling. McNulty confiscated her gun, along with three others."

"She has a *gun*?"

"For the shootout."

Tom pursed his lips. "If she's innocent, the ballistics reports should prove it."

"Right," I said.

Or send her away for life.

Chapter Twenty-Four

I didn't feel like going to work, but Sunday was one of the best days for Belated Rooms. And since the fair was cancelled, I needed to try my best to make up for the lost revenue.

As I cruised along Gulf Boulevard toward the shops on Corey Avenue, I felt conflicted. I desperately needed to talk to Geraldine about the money, but I was also a little bit afraid. Had she killed Orville? If so, would she tell me if I asked? Would I be able to know the truth just by looking into her eyes?

That last one was a non-starter. Honestly, I *never* knew what was going on behind those beady little eyes of hers.

Eager to get our conversation over with, I arrived early. I was surprised to find Geraldine's truck wasn't there, and the front door was locked. By 9 a.m., Geraldine still hadn't arrived. Unlike me, it wasn't like her to be late.

I fished my phone from my purse and called her number. Geraldine didn't pick up. My aggravation turned to worry. Weird thoughts began twirling in my head. Had she skipped town? Had one of her jealous rivals picked her off? Had she eloped with Rooster?

Itching for answers but coming up with scratch, I decided to call Geraldine's sister, Angela Langsbury, who was also my writing teacher. I punched her number and the phone rang once before I remembered I'd skipped Wednesday's class.

"Crap on a cracker!" I clicked off the phone like it was lava. I was in enough trouble as it was.

I realized I needed professional help. And I knew just who to turn to. I locked up the shop and sprinted two blocks down Corey Avenue to the only person who could see through the chaos of my life and give me the answers I sought—if not about Geraldine's future, perhaps mine.

Plus, Wynona Bologna owed me a free palm reading.

. . . .

I DIDN'T TOTALLY BELIEVE in all that psychic stuff. But given the tangled mess Geraldine was in, if I was going to be of any help in keeping her out of jail I was going to have to think outside the box.

I yanked open the door to Your Fortune Foretold and glanced around the tiny, dimly lit shop. It smelled of old books and the scented candles lining the shelves on the walls. In the light streaming through the front window, crocheted dream catchers laced with gemstones glistened as they hung motionless in the silent sanctum of Wynona's metaphysical shop.

"Uh ... hello?" I called out.

From behind a tie-dyed sheet nailed to the wall, a ghostly voice rang out. "Who is it?"

"Uh ... it's me, Val."

"Just a sec!"

The multi-colored curtain nailed to the wall suddenly shifted to one side. A head sporting a blue turban poked out from behind it.

"Oh my," Wynona said. She stepped out from behind the curtain, dressed in a flowing, tri-colored caftan. "You look like you need a reading, girlfriend!"

"That bad, huh?"

"Yep. Big time." Wynona nodded enthusiastically, causing her hoop earrings to sway like pendulums. "And as I recall, I owe you one. So, what's up?"

I glanced at a stack of her business cards lying on the bookshelf. They featured a crystal ball and the intriguing slogan, *Wynona Sees All*.

"I ... I kind of want to know what's going to happen in the immediate future," I said.

"Oh. Then you don't want a palm reading. You want a *crystal ball* reading."

"I do? How much is that?"

She grinned. "Posh. Let's just call it even. I hate owing anybody any-thing. Come have a seat."

Wynona led me into her tiny office. I sat in a chair beside her desk while she pulled a crystal ball from inside a filing cabinet.

"Why do you keep it in there?" I asked. "Are you afraid it will do some kind of secret mojo while you're not looking?"

Wynona cocked her head. "Huh? No. I'm afraid if the sun hits it, it'll start a fire like a magnifying glass."

"Oh."

I glanced around. The place looked more like the storage room at Milly's accounting office than a place for inducing spirits from beyond the realm. Unless they needed their taxes done.

Feeling like it was a mistake to be here, I lifted one butt cheek from the chair to leave. "I um ..."

"Now, sit back and relax," Wynona said, gently pushing me back in-to my chair. She studied me from below two droopy lids smeared with metallic-purple eyeshadow. "Is there something in particular you want to know about?"

Yeah. Did my boss kill Orville Ledbetter?

Not certain whether Wynona had seen the news about Ledbetter, I opted to ask about him using his nickname. "Um ... yes. I want to know about Goggles."

Wynona's eyes grew wide. "Goggles," she whispered, then stared in-to the crystal ball. As I watched, she began to rock back and forth. Then Wynona began to mumble words in a singsong fashion:

"The frogman lurks to his dismay
in pools tinged pink with fury.
His anvil drums and pineal hums
and now he must be buried.
The smell of death is everywhere."

Wynona sat back and blinked. "Well, that was weird."

I grimaced. "You aren't kidding."

She cocked her turban-clad head and studied me. "Did it mean anything to you?"

"Not really. You said 'his anvil drums and pineal hums.' What does that mean?"

"From what I sense, the frogman hears something and his third eye opens."

My nose crinkled. "Third eye?"

"His pineal gland. You know. The one in your brain, right between your eyes."

I gasped. Goggles had been shot between the eyes!

"This pineal gland thing," I said. "It's supposed to bring enlightenment, right?"

Wynona shrugged. "It can. But not always. I've run across more than one individual whose third eye was their butthole."

I smirked. "Copy that. Thanks for the reading."

Wynona smiled. "You're welcome. I hope it helps."

"Me, too."

As I left Your Fortune Foretold, my cellphone rang. It was Langsbury. I cringed and hit the answer button. "Hello?"

"What's your excuse this time?" she said.

"Uh ... sorry about missing class, but I have something even more important to talk to—"

"What's more important than my class?" she hissed.

"Your *sister*. She didn't show up at the shop this morning."

"Didn't she tell you?" Langsbury asked. "She came into some money and took a redeye last night to Vegas."

Chapter Twenty-Five

I couldn't believe it. Had that wily old woman in Crocs gotten the best of me yet again?

Running on gas fumes and rage, I jumped in Shabby Maggie and sped over to the Queen of the Road clubhouse hoping to find some-one—*anyone*—I could talk to about getting some of my money back for sponsoring the fair.

After peeling into the parking lot, I raced into the clubhouse. In a stroke of much-needed luck, I found three familiar faces taking down decorations and picking up the pieces from yesterday's disastrous events.

"What are you doing here?" cotton-haired Lucille demanded upon spotting me coming through the front door.

"I'm really sorry about the fair and everything," I said. "I just came to ... well, I hate to ask, but would it be possible to get back some of the money I paid for sponsoring the fair?"

"*You* paid?" Helga asked. "I thought Geraldine did. Otherwise—"

"No," I said, cutting her off. "It was *my* money."

"Oh," Sylvia nervously tidied her silver bun. "I'm afraid that's im-possible."

My face fell. "Why?"

"I'm sorry," Sylvia said as she walked over to a desk. She unlocked a drawer and pulled out a checkbook. "As you can see, we already gave Geraldine a refund check for $2500."

"She demanded it yesterday afternoon," Lucille said in her tough Jersey accent. "Right after you and Sergeant McNulty left."

Helga shot me a sympathetic smile. "I'm afraid you'll need to ask her about it, dearie."

For a moment I stood speechless staring at the check stub, stunned by my so-called partner's betrayal.

No wonder Geraldine didn't want a lift home yesterday. She was too busy stringing me along for the ride.

• • • •

WITH NO OTHER TRICKS left up my sleeves, I drove back to Belated Rooms feeling as surly as a caged tiger with no claws. While I swept the floor, I wondered why I'd bothered trying to build a business with a woman who couldn't care less about anyone but herself.

I'm here running the shop while Geraldine's throwing my money away on slot machines!

But losing the money wasn't even what hurt the most. It was losing my faith in Geraldine, and perhaps in people as a whole.

Feeling like both a sad-sack and a sap, I glanced up at the shiny new banner for Simply Smashing. Was it just another pipe dream that would never pan out?

If ever there was a time to smash something, it's now.

I walked over to my shop and traded my broom for one of the hammers hanging on the wall. Then I beat the ever-living crap out of a poor, hapless microwave.

• • • •

I WAS HAULING THE MURDERIZED microwave to the dumpster in the alley out back when something rattled around and fell out of it. I looked down at the asphalt and saw something roll to a stop beside my big toe. It was a bullet.

Sweet baby Fritos. Was there anything Geraldine didn't *shoot with that stupid gun of hers?*

I tossed the microwave into the dumpster, then picked up the bullet. Tom had told me last night that ballistics would prove Geraldine's guilt or innocence. But exactly how did all of that work?

Locking the back door behind me, I walked back through the domestic crime scene known as Belated Rooms. When I reached the checkout counter, I plopped onto the stool behind it and gave Tom a call on my cellphone.

"Hey, Val. What's up?"

"Hi! How's your golf game going?"

"That was yesterday." Tom laughed. "Enough with the sweet talk. What do you need?"

I grimaced. Why that man put up with me was the greatest mystery in the history of mysteries. "Um ... what can you tell me about ballistics?"

"If you're asking me to give you specific information on the ballistics reports on the Ledbetter case, no can do, kiddo. Besides, the results won't be in until sometime tomorrow."

"Please? You don't have to give me all the specifics. Just whether the bullet that killed Orville could've come from Geraldine's gun. I really need to know if my current business partner is a murderer. Is that too much to ask?"

I heard Tom blow out a breath. "What type of gun does she have?"

Thank you, thank you, thank you!

"A Junior Commando."

"Two- or four-inch barrel?"

"Um ... it looked pretty short. I'd say two-inch."

"Interesting. A two-inch barrel leaves fewer marks."

"What do you mean?"

"It means ballistics would be harder to trace."

My nose crinkled. "Is that a good thing or a bad thing?"

"That depends on if she's guilty or not."

"Oh."

"Feel like pizza tonight?"

"What?" I suddenly felt too nervous to think. "Oh, sure, Tom. Whatever you want."

In the big scheme of things, at this point what does it matter?

Chapter Twenty-Six

When my cell phone rang Monday afternoon, I nearly jumped out of my skin. I'd been putzing around Belated Rooms all day, waiting for Geraldine to return one of my half-million voicemail messages, and for Tom to call me about the ballistics reports.

I ditched the sinister clown figurine I was about to clobber with my HOJ and snatched up my phone. I checked the display. It was Tom.

"Hi!" I said a tad too enthusiastically. "Did you get the report?"

"I'm fine, too," Tom said. "Thanks for asking."

I winced. "Sorry, I'm just so darned nervous!"

"I get it. But I have some bad news."

I cringed. "Geraldine shot him? I *knew* it!"

"Um ... no, Val. All the test-firing results came back inconclusive. Oddly, there weren't any striation marks on the slug removed from Ledbetter's head."

My brain was too scrambled with worry to register what Tom was saying. "What are you talking about?"

"Basic ballistics," Tom said. "When you fire a gun, grooves inside the barrel make contact with the bullet. Those grooves leave a distinct pattern of scratches on the bullet that are called striations."

"Okay. But how—"

"The striation marks are unique to each gun," Tom continued. "In this case, all three of the guns McNulty collected into evidence were test-fired in a water tank to determine the striation patterns they left on sample bullets."

"Right. I've seen them do that on *Forensic Files*. So, what were the results?"

"That's what I'm trying to explain. The results didn't matter. The bullet recovered from Ledbetter's skull didn't have any discernable striation marks on it to make a comparison."

My nose crinkled. "How is that possible?"

"Actually, it's not as weird as it seems," Tom said. "There's a couple of ways it could happen. For one, the bullet could've been fired from a smoothbore barrel."

"What kind of gun has a smooth barrel?"

"Mostly shotguns."

I gulped.

Winky has a shotgun!

"But Tom, all the guns used in the shootout were handguns. That means none of them could have been the murder weapon, right?"

"Not necessarily. If a handgun's barrel is really corroded, that could cause a lack of ballistic markings. Or if the bullet was made of extremely hard material, like depleted uranium, it could resist striation etching."

I frowned. "What size bullet was it that killed Orville?"

"You mean caliber? It was a .38."

"What kind of bullets does a Junior Commando use?"

Tom laughed. "Whatever kind his Senior Commando lets him."

"Come on, Tom!" I whined. "I'm serious. You know Geraldine's gun is a Junior Commando."

"Take it easy. They use .38s."

"Oh." I winced.

So she's not off the hook.

"What about the Rugers Winky and Sylvia Burns used?" I asked.

"Rugers can use all kinds of ammo, depending on the model. But Winky's Ruger Bearcat Revolver and Burn's Ruger Mark IV both used .22 caliber bullets. Their guns didn't fire the bullet that killed Ledbetter."

"Right," I said. "I guess that leaves Rooster. "Davy Eber said Rooster used a .38 Special in the competition. So, that means the shooter was either him or Geraldine."

"Not necessarily," Tom said. "The caliber matches, but there's no marks on the bullet to compare with Rooster's gun. Besides, any one of them could've switched out weapons to commit the murder."

"Ugh," I groaned. "So the killer could still be anyone."

"At the moment, yes."

Suddenly my phone beeped. I looked at the display. Geraldine was calling me. "Look, Tom. I have to go. I'll call you right back." I clicked off the phone.

"Geraldine?" I yelled into the phone. "What the hell are you up to?"

"Uh, Val? It's still me," Tom said.

I glanced at the phone screen. I'd hung up on Geraldine!

"Aww, crap!" I yelled.

"I love you, too," Tom said.

"Argh! I didn't mean it like that. I missed Geraldine's call."

"Sorry about that."

"It's not your fault." I sighed. "If you guys can't trace the bullet, how are you going to figure out who shot Orville?"

"Alibis and opportunities," Tom said. "Who was in the right place at the right time with the right motive."

"Oh. You know, now that I think about it, I'm not sure anybody participating in the shootout could be at the right place at the right time."

"What do you mean?"

"The way I see it, Orville had to be shot sometime after I left the pool and before the shootout ended. That only leaves maybe ten minutes for the killer to shoot him, hide the second gun, and get to the shootout to compete. That seems way too tight."

"Interesting. Are you sure about the timeline?"

"Well, let's see," I said, doing the math in my head. "Ledbetter didn't get to the pool until after I left. Then it took Saurwein and me about ten minutes to walk the hundred yards or so over to the shootout."

"Ten minutes to walk the length of a football field?" Tom said. "That's too long."

"Uh ... we stopped along the way. To throw softballs at Ferrol Finkerman."

"Excuse me?"

"Finkerman was in a dunking booth and ... anyway, I only got to throw one ball when the first gunshot rang out. Saurwein and I took off for the shootout."

"You went straight there?"

"Yes. Uh, no. I got momentarily stunned by the dump."

"The sight or the smell? Never mind. Go on."

I could almost see Tom's poor face. I was glad I couldn't.

"Anyway," I continued, "by the time we got there, three shots had been fired. Geraldine had finished her round of shooting. Then I watched the other three do their rounds."

"In what order?"

"Um ... Geraldine was done. After her came Winky, then Sylvia, and finally Rooster. Together the three fired nine rounds, making twelve total. That accounts for all shots fired."

"How do you know that?" Tom asked.

"After we found Ledbetter in the pool, McNulty's crew interviewed everyone in the general vicinity. No one said they heard any gunshots except the twelve fired during the shootout."

"I see," Tom said. "Val, you'd be surprised the percentage of the general public that can't count to twelve. Besides, in the excitement of the fair, who would be keeping track?"

My nose crinkled. "You think we might've missed a shot?"

"You must've. With that high a number, it's possible. But from what you told me, only three shots had been fired by the time Geraldine finished her round, correct?"

"Yes."

"Three is an easy number to keep track of," Tom said. "And since Geraldine was at the shootout when you got there, she couldn't have shot Ledbetter."

"Oh my word!" I yelped. "You're right! She couldn't!"

"Unless she had someone else do it for her."

"Oh, Tom. Why would you say that about her?"

"Me?" Tom laughed. "You're the one who keeps telling me she'd do anything for money. Have you talked to her about it?"

"No."

"Why not?"

"Because she hasn't been returning my voicemails. That's why I tried to ditch you to grab her call."

"She isn't at work with you?"

"No."

"Why not?"

I grimaced. "Because she took off for Vegas right after the fair shut down on Saturday."

"Really," Tom said. "Is anyone else missing in action?"

"Uh ... Rooster. Nobody's seen him either."

"How well do those two know each other?"

"I don't know," I said.

"I guess I should tell you the slug you found in the microwave yesterday is also a .38. And it was mangled almost as badly as the slug they pulled from Orville's skull. Do you have any idea who might've fired it?"

I grimaced. "I couldn't say for sure."

But I'm gonna find out.

Chapter Twenty-Seven

When I hung up the phone with Tom, I had more doubts about Geraldine than ever!

I'd have bet good money I'd only heard three gunshots by the time Geraldine finished her turn at the shootout competition. She, Sylvia Burns, and Winky had all been present at the time. I'd seen them with my own eyes.

If Tom's three-shot theory eliminated Geraldine as Orville's *outright* killer, it also eliminated Sylvia Burns and Winky (not that he was ever really in it).

But try as I might, I couldn't recall seeing Rooster right then. He'd been last to shoot. And he'd still been mowing the grounds when I'd left the pool area. The timing was tight, but of the four shootout competitors, he was the only one with a chance to pull off shooting Orville.

But why would he?

I stared out the front window of the shop, wracking my brain for a motive. Did Geraldine hire Rooster to kill Orville? Did she threaten to terminate his mowing contract at the trailer park if he didn't do it? Is that what he'd meant when he'd told me he had an arrangement with the "powers that be"?

I shook my head. A lousy mowing contract seemed like mighty poor compensation for murdering somebody. But then again, people have done a lot worse for a lot less. At least, that's what Joe Kenda says on *Homicide Hunter*.

But why would Geraldine want Orville dead?

Oh, yeah. She was dating him.

• • • •

I'D JUST FINISHED LEAVING Geraldine another voicemail when the front door to the shop squeaked open like a castrated toad. I braced for having to deal with a customer. But it turned out to be Winky, toting a box full of junk in his arms.

"Hey!" I called out. "You're supposed to *buy* junk here, not dump it and run."

Winky laughed as he walked up and set the box on top of the checkout counter. "Thought you might be needin' some more stuff for your new place. I heard ol' Milly already smashed the tar outta half your shop."

I smirked. "Bad news travels fast around here." I peeked inside the box. "This looks like prime hammer material. Thanks!"

Winky shook his head. "Don't thank me. Thank Winnie. She told me if I didn't get shed of some of the crap in the garage, she was gonna make me live out back in the shed."

"At least you'd still be alive, unlike poor old Orville."

"True that," Winky said with a grin. "Gotta count your blessin's, even when they's blessin' outs."

"Exactly." I pulled an old vase from Winky's donation box and studied it, trying to appear nonchalant. "Hey Winky. Do you think someone would kill somebody over losing a mowing contract?"

Winky rubbed his stubbly chin. "Maybe. My cousin Earl killed a whole nest a wasps for a quarter."

"When you were kids?"

"Nope. Last week."

My nose crinkled. I'd wanted to play it coy with Winky, but the stakes were too high.

"Winky, you know the shootout at the fair?"

"The one where I won me this all-you-can-eat sushi from the Poke Corral food truck?" he asked, whipping the coupon from his shirt pocket.

"Yes, Winky. That one."

"What about it?" he asked, tucking the coupon back into his pocket.

"You were near Geraldine when she shot at her target, right?"

"Yessum."

"How many gunshots had you heard when she was done?"

"Three. Why?"

"Just a theory I'm working on."

"About who done in Orville Redenbacher?"

"Ledbet—never mind. Yes. With four people shooting three shots each, that's twelve gunshots total."

"If'n you say so, Chief."

Lord. Tom was right.

"Winky, if there were only 12 rounds fired, how could somebody fire a shot at Orville without anybody hearing it?"

"Oh, I know!" Winky said excitedly. "If they shot him from outer space!"

"What?"

"Ol' Goober once told me that sound requires something to travel on, like air or water. Without it, there wouldn't be nothing to transmit the sound waves." Winky beamed proudly. "Either that, or there wasn't nobody around to hear it."

"There were plenty of people around at the fair," I said.

Winky gasped. "Then the killer must a been a space bandit!"

"Perhaps," I said, stifling an eye roll. "Wait. Could it have been a ricochet bullet from Geraldine's or Rooster's gun?"

"I guess so. If'n a space alien could ... wait a minute. Why couldn't it a been *my* gun? Or that old lady's with the silver bun?"

"Because your and Sylvia's guns were .22 caliber. Tom said the bullet that killed Orville was a .38."

"Oh," Winky said. "They sure got the ballistics back fast."

"Mainly because there was nothing to make a comparison with. Tom said the bullet that killed Orville didn't have any markings on it."

Winky scratched his head. "How can that be so?"

"I dunno. Tom said a bunch of stuff about corroded barrels and depleted uranium bullets."

"Bullets can deplete your cranium?" Winky asked, his eyes wide.

I sighed. "Only if you've got something in there in the first place. Don't worry. You're in no danger."

"Well, that's good to know."

"But here's something that's *not* so good to know," I said. "It's looking like the only possible suspects are Geraldine and Rooster."

"Or that space bandit."

"Right. But we can't exactly snoop on a *spaceman*, now can we?"

Winky wagged his eyebrows. "Are you sayin' we need to do us another stakeout?"

I shrugged. "Would you settle for a break-in?"

Winky laughed. "Where at?"

"Orville's trailer."

Winky shook his head solemnly. "That poor ol' feller."

"Yeah. I got a feeling he won't mind if we look around his place."

"Prolly not. What time?"

"Tonight at seven. Can you make it?"

"Does a pig poop in a pen?"

"I need you to take this seriously, Winky. If we're gonna prove Geraldine didn't do this, the onus is on *us*."

Winky's freckled nose crinkled. "Eww. I don't want nobody's onus on me!"

Chapter Twenty-Eight

"**G**ood grief, Winky!" I said as he swerved from side to side down the main street running through the center of Queen of the Road Trailer Park.

"Sorry," he said. "Where I'm from, side-swiping potholes is a survival skill."

"Over there!" I said as Winky hit one big enough to make me bounce in the van seat. "That one's Orville Ledbetter's doublewide."

"I'm on it," Winky said, then hung a sharp left into the driveway. The old green trailer was so close to the pool that even in the fading light of dusk, we could make out the yellow crime scene tape still surrounding the crime scene.

"Just perzackly what are we here for?" Winky asked, shoving the gear shift into park.

I shot him what I hoped was a look of confidence. "A hunch."

Winky's eyes grew wide. "Orville Redenbacher was a *hunchback*?"

"No, Winky. The *other* kind of hunch. I've got a feeling there's more to Orville than meets the eye."

Winky giggled. "Which eye you talkin' about? I heard he had three."

I stared at him like a schoolteacher about to reach for her ruler. "Are you done with the corny jokes, young man?"

Winky slumped in his seat. "Yes, ma'am."

"Good. Kill the headlights and listen up. Remember our last stakeout we heard those women talking about how Orville came to the pool wearing goggles?"

"Yes, ma'am."

"One of them said he always brought a dirty duffel bag with him."

Winky nodded. "Yep, I recollect that. So?"

I grabbed my flashlight from the floorboard. "Well, as far as I can tell, nobody's bothered to look for Orville's bag."

Winky cocked his head. "Why would they?"

"I've got a theory. Follow along. Now, Orville was supposed to be in the shootout. You took his place."

"Yep." Winky reached for his shirt pocket. "That's how I won me this here all-you-can-eat—"

I slapped his hand. "Why in the world did you bring that with you?"

"Come on, Val-Pal. You never know when the Poke Corral truck's gonna pull up."

I willed myself not to bonk Winky on the head with my flashlight. "Right. Anyway, what if Orville carried his gun in his duffel bag? You know, the way Geraldine carries hers in her purse?"

"Oh! I know! Then it'd be a *man purse*, not a duffel bag."

I sighed and wondered where I'd gone so wrong in my life.

"Okay, sure, Winky. But follow me now. Orville always took that duffel bag with him to the pool. But it wasn't there when they found his body. What if somebody shot Orville with his own gun, then hid the weapon along with his duffel bag?"

I could almost hear the gears shift inside Winky's noggin and his slow train finally pulled into the station.

"Lawdy mercy, Val-Pal!" he said. "We need to find us that man-purse duffel bag!"

"Exactly." I clicked open the passenger door. "Now follow me. We're about to commence Operation Duffel Kerfuffle."

Winky's brow furrowed. "Is he the one what makes the man purses?"

• • • •

"JIMINY JOSEPHAT!" WINKY yelped as we stepped inside Orville's trailer and I shone my flashlight. "This place's dirtier than a hog's behind! What'cha call it when somebody don't throw nothin' out and lives in filthy squalor?"

"Bachelorhood?" I quipped.

"No, that ain't it."

"Hoarding," I said. "It's called hoarding."

"Whatever you call it, how're we supposed to find anything in this mess?"

"Shh! Keep your voice down. The neighbors might hear us." I stumbled through the cramped living room to the kitchen. Through the haze of my flashlight, I could see the countertops were stacked to the upper cabinets in TV dinner cartons, empty beer cans, and takeout bags.

"Watch out," I said as Winky ambled up behind me.

Winky chuckled. "How dangerous could this place be? It's an old fogey retirement home."

Suddenly a loud *crack* rang out in the kitchen. Winky, arms flailing, fell-face first to the floor beside my feet.

"Winky!" I shrieked, my eyes darting around in the dim light, searching for his assailant. "Are you all right?"

"Yeah," he said, getting up on his knees. "Just got tripped up on this here tree branch." He held up a small limb that had cracked in half when he'd stepped on it.

I shook my head. "Why in the world would Orville have a tree branch in his kitchen?" I asked as Winky hauled himself to standing.

He glanced around. "My guess? He's got hisself a pet squirrel. Or maybe a possum. Or one a them fancy iguanas. Or maybe a—"

"I take it back," I said. "I don't want to know."

"Have it your way. But I don't see no duffel bag in here."

"Let's check the rest of the place. And watch your step!"

* * * *

TWENTY MINUTES LATER, the only thing I'd found inside Orville's hoarder trailer was a pile of skid-marked undershorts and a spider in the tub that was as big as my hand.

"Let's get out of here," I said, tugging Winky by the arm. "And put that beer opener down. No souvenirs!"

"Ol' Goggles ain't gonna miss it," Winky said. "There's so much junk in here a feller could get lost in it."

I gasped. "That's it!"

"Huh?" Winky grunted.

"Lost items. Where do they end up?"

Winky shrugged. "In Heaven?"

"No! People *turn them in*." I peeked through the blinds covering a dirty window. On the other side of the pool, lights were glowing inside the clubhouse. "Come on, Winky. Let's go see if the clubhouse has a Lost and Found."

"I know they do," Winky said. "I put somethin' in there the other day."

"Good. Let's go!"

Like a pair of bumbling cat burglars, we snuck out of Orville's trailer and scrambled across the lawn separating it from the pool and clubhouse.

"Lay low," I said to Winky as I peeked into the sliding glass doors.

"What are they doing?" Winky asked.

"Looks to me like they're playing pinochle."

Winky grinned. "I always wanted to learn how to play that. Let's go in!"

He reached for the door. I slapped his hand away. "We can't be spotted by anyone. Operation Duffel Kerfuffle, remember?"

"Oh, yeah!"

"Is there a side door to this place?" I asked.

"Yep. Right over yonder. Leads into the liberry and the Lost & Found closet."

"Perfect. You lead the way."

"You got it, Chief."

Winky turned and crept along the side of the clubhouse, then turned the corner. It led to a small breezeway lined with benches and ashtrays. "This here's the smokin' section," he said.

"Thanks for clarifying that," I said. "Now, where's the side door?"

"Right cheer." Winky pulled the doorknob. The door opened. "Ha! It ain't even locked!"

"Wait!" I yelped. But it was too late. Winky flung open the door. It squealed like a rusty hinge in a slasher movie.

"Shh!" I hissed.

"That wasn't me," Winky said. "It was the door!"

"Ugh! I know. Just ... try to be quiet, okay? People are right over there on the other side of this L-shaped room!"

"Don't get your panties in a wad," Winky said as I followed him into a small wing off the main room. It was crammed with books and games for the residents to check out. In the middle of the wall was a door that read, Lost & Found.

Score!

"See?" Winky said, pointing to it. "There it is."

"Yes, I see that," I said. "So open it."

Winky pulled the door open. Sitting on a shelf was a filthy, thread-bare duffel bag.

"Oh my gosh!" I said. "That's got to be it!"

Winky frowned. "It cain't be."

"Why not?"

"Cause that's the same one I stuck in here when I came back from the shootout. I found it stuffed in the tiki hut. I put it in here 'cause I needed the space for the donuts."

I really should've won an Academy Award for maintaining my composure. "Winky, why didn't you tell me that earlier?"

"You said you was lookin' for a *duffel* bag. That there's a *gym* bag."

So much for that Academy Award. My patience gone, I snatched the bag from the shelf like it was the last life raft on the Titanic. As I swung the ragged thing down off the shelf, the bottom fell out of it. A set of swim goggles and an open carton of bullets tumbled out. The carton hit the terrazzo floor, scattering gold metallic ammo all over the place.

"Crap!" I hissed.

But before I could even bend down to start picking them up, a woman's voice rang out, "What's going on over there?"

"Um ...," I said.

Winky grinned. "Why howdy there. We was just lookin' for Duffel's Kerfuffel, ma'am!"

The woman gasped. "Mabel! Call the police!"

Chapter Twenty-Nine

"Fremden," McNulty said as he came through the clubhouse door at Queen of the Road Trailer Park. "I should've known."

"I can explain," I said, cringing from guilt and stupidity.

"Those two were trying to steal that gym bag out of the Lost & Found closet!" the woman who'd nabbed us said.

Winky shot me a look. "Told you it was a *gym* bag."

McNulty glanced over at the dirty, worn-out bag lying atop a folding table. "Well, I can see why nobody claimed it," he said. He turned and stared at me. "What's going on here, Fremden?"

"I just had a thought," I said. "But I didn't want to bother you with it unless it panned out."

"A thought?" he said. "About the Ledbetter Case?"

"Yes, sir. I just was thinking that whoever shot Goggles could've stowed the gun in his duffel ... *gym* bag. You see, according to some of the women here, Orville always brought that bag with him to the pool—"

"She's right," the woman said. "He never showed up without his bag."

"I can second that," a man's voice sounded. It belonged to Davy Eber.

McNulty studied me for a second, then nodded. "Go on, Fremden."

"Well, sir, when you found Orville shot in the pool, you cordoned off the area, right?"

"Yes."

"Did you find a gym bag?"

McNulty's skeptical look skipped a beat. "No. But how do you know this bag belonged to Orville?"

"Oh, that's his bag all right," the woman said. "Who else would want to touch it?"

McNulty's nose crinkled. "Fair point. But how did you know it would be in the Lost & Found?"

"Oh!" Winky said, raising his hand. "On account a I put it in there!"

"Did you now," McNulty said, letting out a big sigh.

"It's a long story, sir," I said.

"Save it, for now," McNulty said. "Let's first see if there's anything to this, or if I can go home and finish eating my dinner." He walked over to the table where the gym bag sat. "What's with the box of .38 ammo here?"

"It fell out when I picked up the bag," I said. "The bottom's pretty worn out."

McNulty donned a pair of gloves and picked up a slug lying amidst the shiny gold cartridges. "A spent bullet?"

"Maybe he saved it as a souvenir," Winky said.

"He *was* a hoarder," I said.

"Uh-huh." McNulty set the bullet down, unzipped the bag, and looked inside. He pulled out a small, red notebook. When he opened it, his eyebrows rose an inch.

"What is it?" Winky asked. "Devil doodles like Val-Pal makes of Geraldine?"

I cringed. "It was just the one time—"

"Not exactly," McNulty said, cutting me off. "But close." He turned the notebook around to show us a page. It featured a very unflattering doodle of a large woman in a bathing suit—minus the top.

Eber gasped. "That's spot on a match for Gladys Farnsworth!"

The woman who'd called the cops on us gasped. "That creep! I knew Orville was a pervert!"

McNulty shook his head and laid the notebook on the table. He reached into the bag again. This time he pulled out a gun.

It was my turn to gasp. "I was right!"

"Don't jump to conclusions," McNulty said. "We don't even know if this gun can be fired. It's in pretty rough shape."

"Let me have a look," Davy Eber said. "It's a Commando."

"Like Geraldine's gun?" I asked.

"Yes, only it's got a four-inch barrel."

"Takes a .38?" McNulty asked.

"Yes," Eber said. "But the barrel's got to be the most corroded I've seen in 30 years of buying and trading."

"Too corroded to work?" I asked.

Eber examined the barrel, then gave it a sniff. "Huh. Maybe. Smells like it's been recently fired."

I stared at the pitted metal revolver. "Um ... what could cause a barrel to corrode like that?" I asked.

"Not your normal wear and tear, that's for sure," Eber said. "No, this is the kind of etching you find with long-term exposure to abrasive chemicals like uric acid and chlorine."

"Like in pool water?" McNulty asked.

"Sure," Eber said.

I groaned inside.

Or from being stashed inside a toilet tank?

Oh, Geraldine. What have you done?

Chapter Thirty

"What does all this mean?" the woman who'd called the cops on us asked McNulty.

"Nothing I can comment on at the moment," McNulty said. "Fremden? A word?"

McNulty pulled me to the side. "Finding another gun isn't going to prove anything. The bullet that killed Orville had no usable marks for ballistic comparison, as you well know."

"Uh, yes sir," I said, staring at his shoes. "But don't blame Tom—"

"So he *did* share that information with you," McNulty said. "Never mind. We'll deal with that later. Right now, I'm more concerned with you going out on your own and tampering with evidence!"

"But sir, all we did was find the bag. Winky stowed it away in the Lost & Found closet after he discovered it by the tiki hut. But that was *after* the shootout. So Orville probably carried it there himself."

"Excuse me," the pinochle playing woman said, tapping McNulty on the shoulder. "Could Orville have shot himself?"

"And put his gun back into his gym bag?" Eber scoffed. "Hardly."

"Unless someone found him and stashed the gun to cover up the suicide," McNulty said.

"Why would they do that?" I asked.

"A lot of life insurance policies don't pay out for suicide," the woman said. "All the women around here know that."

McNulty frowned. "Fair point. I'll send a detective to check out Ledbetter's trailer. Perhaps we'll find a money trail."

"Good luck with that," Winky said. "The only trail we found inside that place was a pile a rat droppin's."

McNulty's eagle eyes soared down on Winky. "And just exactly how would you know that?"

"'Cause we done been through it," Winky said, elbowing me.

"We didn't remove anything," I blurted. "We were only looking for the bag."

"Operation Duffel Kerfuffle," Winky said. "Only maybe we should a called it Operation Slim Gym, on account of the old bag."

"Excuse me, sonny," the pinochle playing woman said. "Who're you calling an old bag?"

• • • •

BY SOME MIRACLE, MCNULTY released me and Winky on our own idiotic recognizance, with a warning for us to stay out of his business. I excused myself and used the opportunity to go to the ladies' room. I didn't tell anyone, but I wanted to check the toilet tank Winky had fixed on Saturday.

I lifted the lid on the tank in the middle stall. Nothing.

If Geraldine had stashed a gun in there, she hadn't put it back. Either there never was a gun in the tank, or she'd found a new hiding place.

Like Orville's dirty old gym bag.

As we walked to Winky's van, I tried calling Geraldine. But for the millionth time, it clicked over to her voicemail message;

"Tag. You're it."

I sighed and climbed into the van, trying to imagine what Geraldine was doing at this very moment. Probably pulling the handle on a slot machine with my last dollar.

I smiled wistfully. I had to hand it to her. The woman was in her seventies and living it up on the lam in Vegas. As far as happy endings for murderers went, I had to admit it wasn't half bad.

• • • •

WHEN WINKY DROPPED me off at my house I figured it was around midnight. But when I checked the clock, it was only 9:30.

Forget the time. Where did my *energy* go?

I snuck down the hallway to find Tom already in bed. The TV was on, and he was lightly snoring. As I climbed into bed, I felt Tom's arms pull me toward him. A warm wave of relief fell over me like a comfy blanket. At least we could grow old and decrepit together.

I tried to sleep. But all I could think about was Geraldine.

Chapter Thirty-One

I *was up to my waist in hot water in Winky's above-ground swimming pool, arm-wrestling my ginger-haired pal for the last cruller in a dented donut box. All around us, frogs as big as sea turtles were playing bongos, drinking margaritas, and croaking out raspy tunes ....*

I snorted myself awake, then belched like one of those frogs in my dream.

Ugh! I really shouldn't have eaten that Circle J burrito on the way home last night.

I sat up in bed, causing an image to tumble to the forefront of my brain like a bag of dirty laundry. It was Wynona. She was in her blue turban, rocking back and forth, gazing into that crystal ball of hers. The words she'd said to me a few days ago sounded like a scratched record playing in my mind:

The frogman lurks to his dismay
in pools tinged pink with fury.
His anvil drums and pineal hums
and now he must be buried.
The smell of death is everywhere.

Even though I was still groggy from sleep, in hindsight most of what she'd said to me a few days ago somehow made sense now.

The frogman had to be Orville in his goggles. He was found in a swimming pool. And the pink tinge had to be blood seeping from the wound where he'd been shot. The fury? His perverted behavior pissed all the old ladies off.

As for the anvil and drum, they were the parts of the ear that made hearing possible. Had Orville heard the gunshot before his pineal gland was obliterated by that bullet between his eyes?

The gunshot had killed him. And, of course, he now had to be buried. But what about that last line? It didn't seem to match the poetic rhythm of Wynona's singsong words;

The smell of death is everywhere.

Could Wynona have been referring to Orville himself? Judging by his trailer, the guy lived in filth. The women who called him a pervert also said he'd left grease stains in the pool every time he got in.

The thought made my stomach churn.

But wait ... maybe the smell was coming from the nearby dump, Mount Trashmore ....

"What 'cha thinking about?" Tom asked.

I glanced up to find him watching me from the doorframe of our bedroom.

"Nothing!" I blurted. "Except that cappuccino in your hand ... oh, and *you*, of course."

"Nice save." Tom grinned, walked over, and handed me the cup. "The weather report says heavy thunderstorms today. Maybe even possible tornado warnings. I gotta go. Be careful out there today. Okay?"

"I will. You do the same."

"Always."

Tom kissed me lightly on the lips. As I watched him disappear out the bedroom door, a sudden thought made me gasp.

The smell of death is everywhere.

Could Geraldine and Rooster be dead, too?

• • • •

THE SKY WAS A BRUISED patchwork of deep blues and purples as I drove to the shop in Shabby Maggie. It appeared as ominous as the fact that Geraldine had been gone for three days without a word. From what I'd heard, Las Vegas could be a dangerous place for lone travelers.

As I pulled onto Corey Avenue, huge raindrops began to spatter the windshield. I squealed into a parking spot in front of Belated

Rooms and hit the button on the cabriolet top. It grumbled and be-grudgingly jerked its way up and over the backseat. By the time it reached over my head, I was half soaked.

With a final groan, the top finally landed on the chrome rim of the windshield. I locked the ragtop in place and stared at the dingy thrift shop through the rain. I hoped it would let up soon so I could make a mad dash for the door.

As I sat in the steamy car watching rain pelt the windshield, I thought about Geraldine. I was genuinely worried about her. Sure, she was a surly old cuss. But as I'd gotten to know her, I realized she was the kind of woman who did her dirty deeds in the open and her kind ones in secret.

Even though she was always cussing and complaining about me to my face, behind my back she'd willed me her business. Ornery as she was, she'd given me a chance at employment when nobody else would. She'd even agreed to let me start my own business inside her shop, without hesitation.

Geraldine had become much more than just a business partner. In a way, she'd become my new role model. That salty old woman was a cork in a storm. She always managed to find a way to get her head back above water. I was envious of her spunk, and her unconventional, do-as-she-darn-well-pleased attitude.

Geraldine might not own much, but she definitely owned her life.

As I stared at Belated Rooms through the rain, I realized something else about Geraldine. She spoke my love language.

Our constant battle of wits reminded me of my relationship with my true mother. We shared a love that came packed with sandspurs. Certainly prickly, but not meant to do any real damage. I could see Glad on that lounge chair in the sun doling out advice behind bug-eyed sunglasses and a red-lipstick grin.

*If you're observant enough, kiddo, people will tell on them-
selves.*

In her own way Geraldine had told me she loved me. I couldn't
imagine her intentionally hurting someone. At least, I couldn't until
she stole my money and ran off to Vegas with it. She'd crossed a line I
didn't think she would. If she could do that to me, could she have killed
Orville—and maybe Rooster, too?

No. I refused to believe it.

Despite McNulty's warning for me to keep out of the case, I needed
to prove Geraldine's innocence—before he proved her guilt.

Glad's voice bubbled up in my mind;

*When someone tells you that you can't do something, you can
be pretty dang sure you're on the right track.*

I sat straight up in the driver's seat. There was nothing more I could
do about Geraldine or Orville at the moment, but I *could* try and track
down what happened to Rooster.

I turned the ignition on Shabby Maggie, got the windshield wipers
slapping, and headed for Queen of the Road Trailer Park.

Chapter Thirty-Two

It's a known fact that Florida's weather is some of the most unpredictable on the planet. Out of a clear, cloudless sky, a thunderstorm can come rolling in within minutes. It can be raining in your front yard but not your backyard. And, on rare occasions, the air has been known to turn light pink, blue, or green at the end of a summer downpour.

As I sped east in Shabby Maggie away from the rain and toward Queen of the Road Trailer Park, the sky in that direction looked blue—but all I could see was red.

Part of me was hopping mad at Geraldine for blowing the money I'd given her on another one of her Vegas benders. And part of me was burning mad at myself for being gullible enough to fall for her tricks once again.

Still, as I turned onto Haines Road, I found myself hoping against hope that I was wrong about Geraldine being a thief and a murderer. The evidence was mounting that she'd played a part in killing Orville. Had Rooster been her accomplice? After he'd done the deed, had she killed Rooster, too?

I hit the gas. The roar of Maggie's glass-pack mufflers sounded like an anguished plea to the Universe.

Please don't let the killer be Geraldine!

When I reached the sign for the trailer park, I swerved into the parking lot of the clubhouse—and did a doubletake. Like an answered prayer, I spotted Rooster unloading his riding mower. I zoomed over, then hit the brakes and screeched to a halt beside him.

"Rooster!" I squealed. "You're not dead!"

Rooster laughed. "Was I supposed to be?"

"Um ... no. It's just that we couldn't find you Saturday after the shootout. The police want to question you about—"

"Orville Ledbetter," Rooster said, finishing my sentence. "The police called me. I went to the station and handed in my gun on Monday."

"Oh. I didn't know."

"Should you? You're not a cop. Are you?"

I blanched. "Of course not!"

"Good. And I'm not a killer." He wagged his eyebrows at me. "I'm a lover instead. Interested?"

My nose crinkled imagining how many hen-house doors this cock-of-the-walk had darkened. "Uh ... no thanks."

"You sure about that, pretty lady?"

"Totally sure," I said. "I'm curious. Did you have that kind of 'arrangement' with Geraldine?"

Rooster's lascivious gaze evaporated. "Ha!" he laughed. "Geraldine? That woman would hardly pay me for *junk for her shop*. If there wasn't a profit in it, she wouldn't lay out a dime."

My cell phone rang. "Gotta go. This is my *cop* boyfriend calling."

"I see. Well, I better get to work, then. No hard feelings. With me, it's just a numbers game."

"Thanks for making me feel so special," I said, watching him start the engine on his mower. He waved, shifted gears and took off for the grassy field beside the clubhouse.

Rooster was no Romeo, but he'd been honest about his intentions, and not pushy. As I watched him go, I felt fairly certain the only thing he'd mown down lately was grass. But then again, looks could be deceiving.

I clicked the *answer* button on my cellphone. "Hey, Tom. What's up?"

"Wanted to give you a heads up. There's a tornado watch."

"Oh." I glanced up at the blue sky. "Okay. Thanks. It's pretty clear right now where I am."

"And where's that?"

"Um ... Geraldine's trailer park."

"What are you doing—"

"Um ... any news on the Ledbetter case?" I blurted over him. "I'm worried about Geraldine. I'm going to stop by her trailer and see if she's home yet."

"Right," Tom said. But he didn't sound convinced. "We got some news on the gun from Ledbetter's gym bag. Forensics showed it hadn't been fired recently. So that rules out Ledbetter shooting himself with it and someone else covering it up."

"Thanks. I guess the gym bag turned out to be a dead end."

"Not necessarily," Tom said. "When Brady and his crew swept the pool area on Saturday afternoon, they found two spent bullet casings in the grass. They matched the make and manufacturer of the bullets found in Ledbetter's gym bag."

I gulped. "They came from the same carton of bullets?"

"Yes. Whoever had access to the bullets in Ledbetter's gym bag is probably our killer. And given the location of the spent cartridges, they must've fired at Ledbetter from the grass just outside the pool area."

"Tom, why would the killer steal Orville's bullets but not his gun? That doesn't make any sense."

"If the criminal mind were always logical, we'd solve cases a lot quicker," Tom said. "Ledbetter's gun was too corroded to actually work. My guess is the killer knew that."

"So they were a gun expert?" I asked.

Like Davy Eber?

"Possibly. But I'd say just about anyone familiar with weapons could tell his gun was beyond the ability to function."

"Thanks, Tom. So, what about Rooster's gun?"

"Rooster?"

"Uh ... Carl Menendez. He told me he handed in his .38 Special for testing yesterday."

"Not sure about that. Hold on. I've got a call coming in over the radio."

While I waited on hold, I thought about what an incorrigible skin-flint Geraldine was. Could she have lifted a few bullets off Orville for her practice sessions and accidentally shot him with one? Or worse yet, could she have intentionally shot him?

"Val?" Tom said, coming back on the line. "I've got to go. There's been a tornado touchdown by Corey Avenue."

"Holy crap! Is Belated Rooms involved?"

"I don't know. But that reminds me. McNulty said they found Ledbetter's will during a search of his trailer. All of his assets were shifted to Geraldine two days before his death. You still haven't heard from her?"

"No," I said as my throat tightened like a knot. And it was looking more and more like I never would again.

Chapter Thirty-Three

Someone shot Orville from the grassy area just outside the pool. Yet no one reported hearing a gunshot. The only person I *couldn't* eliminate was Geraldine. Had she hidden a silencer in the toilet tank?

Oh, Geraldine. What have you done?

I left the clubhouse and pulled up to Geraldine's trailer in a panic. After banging on her door for five minutes with no answer, I was at my wits' end.

Then I thought about Winky. He'd left the pool area with Geraldine to go to the shootout. He'd been with her during the timeframe Orville had been killed. Surely he could alibi her, couldn't he? I hopped back in Shabby Maggie and called him on my cell phone.

"Hey, Val-Pal!"

"Hey, Winky. Look, I'm trying to figure out if Geraldine shot Orville or not."

"Oh. Good golly. I don't see how she could a managed it."

My heart soared. "You were with her the whole time after she left the pool for the shootout, right?"

"Well, lemme see. That Orville feller wasn't in the pool when Ms. G. hauled me over to the shootout. And then I was with her signing all them papers before Eber could let me hold that sweet Ruger Bearcat Revolver with a wooden grip."

"So Geraldine has an airtight alibi! Did you tell McNulty that on Saturday?"

"Nope. It never came up. But now that I think about it, while I was busy fillin' out paperwork, she could a snuck off and got a shot in edgewise."

Oh, crap.

My phone beeped. I was getting another call. "Thanks, Winky. I gotta go."

"Okie dokie. Be careful out there. Heard there was tornadoes around."

"You stay safe, too!" I clicked off his call and picked up the next one. "Hello?"

"Fremden?" I heard McNulty say.

"Yes, sir."

"I've been trying to locate your business partner, Geraldine Jiggles. She's not answering her phone. Do you know her whereabouts?"

"I heard she went to Vegas, sir."

"Why doesn't that surprise me?" he said.

"You and me both, sir."

"I hope she's having better luck there than she's having here."

"What do you mean?" I asked.

"Nothing. But if you hear from her, have her call me immediately."

• • • •

I TURNED THE KEY IN the ignition and stomped the gas pedal. Shabby Maggie roared to life, echoing my primal scream.

Why is it that every time I almost get my life together, it falls apart spectacularly?

I reached for the gear to shift, ready to peel out of the Queen of the Road Trailer Park like a broken bat out of hell. But that blasted niggling feeling of hope kept rising up inside me was like a cork in the ocean. I decided to call Geraldine one more time.

I got her voicemail.

"That's it!" I yelled. "I give up!"

I mashed the *end call* button so hard on my cell phone it chirped.

Then it began dialing another number. "Ack!" Before I could stop it, Geraldine's sister, Angela Langsbury, answered the phone.

"What do you want, Fremden?" she hissed by way of a greeting.

"I'm just calling to check on Geraldine. Have you heard from her?"

"Yes. She took a redeye flight back last night. I'm sitting at the airport waiting for her now."

"That's great," I said. "Please have her call me as soon as she gets in, okay?"

"Why?"

"I need to update her on a few things."

"What kind of things?"

I grimaced. If I told Langsbury the real reasons—that I wanted to shake her sister down for my money and the truth about Orville—Geraldine would never call. I decided to improvise.

"Tell Geraldine the thrift shop's been hit by a tornado."

"What?" Langsbury said. "If this is some ploy to get out of class tomorrow—"

"It's not. I'm on my way to check out the damage for myself. Please. Have her call me!"

Then I hung up before she had a chance to weasel the truth out of me.

Chapter Thirty-Four

When I pulled up to Corey Avenue, trash and debris was everywhere—but the sky, now a bright blue, had already forgotten all about the devastation it had left behind.

Up and down the quaint little main street, glass storefronts were cracked or completely blown out. Outdoor café tables and chairs lay mangled where they'd been tossed around like tumbleweeds. I spotted the sandwich board from the Friendly Fish dangling from atop the State Theater's towering Art Deco movie marquee.

"You can't come in here, ma'am," a young police officer said as I ducked under the yellow caution tape that cordoned off the road from gawkers and looters.

"It's me," I said to Officer Brady.

"Oh, Ms. Fremden," he said. "I'm sorry about your shop. You can go ahead, but please be careful of all the glass."

"Thank you, Officer Brady. I will."

As I picked my way toward the shop, I began to recognize some of the bits of household junk that had been in the display window of Geraldine's thrift shop. Leaning up against a wall I spotted a two-foot-tall letter that had come off someone's signage. The broken letter D looked a little too familiar.

I glanced up at the wall above the blown-out storefront window of Belated Rooms. The remaining all-caps letters of our sign now read: LATE ROO.

My heart sank. Like Geraldine, I'd poured everything into this place. Now it was gone. But thanks to Geraldine, we no longer had the money to make a comeback.

As I made my way through the maze of debris toward the remnants of Belated Rooms, I heard the dull clack of footsteps behind me. I turned to see Geraldine scurrying along the sidewalk in my direction, her sister Angela Langsbury hot on her heels.

"Geraldine!" I yelled as she drew closer. "I need to talk to you."

But the old woman blew past me toward her beloved thrift shop as if she hadn't seen or heard me. I rushed up to her as she frantically unlocked the shop's front door.

"Barney!" she hollered as she pushed the door open and rushed past the tangle of merchandise littering the floor. "Barney! You're okay!"

"Barney?" I asked, scampering up behind her. "What are you talking about? Who's Barney?"

Geraldine lunged toward the black antique cash register. It was still perched on the broken plexiglass checkout counter. "Barney!" she said, hugging the huge hulk of metal. "You're the only one I can rely on!"

"Excuse me?" I said, indignation rising. "I've been the one taking care of the shop while you ran off to Vegas!"

"And look at it!" Geraldine said. "This place is a wreck!"

"What?" I gasped. "I can't stop a tornado!"

Geraldine's distressed face suddenly softened. "No, you can't. Just like I couldn't stop a hurricane."

I frowned. "What are you talking about?"

"Barney's been with Geraldine through thick and thin," Langsbury said, walking over and standing beside her sister.

"I don't understand," I said.

"Barney's the only thing that survived Hurricane Andrew," Langsbury said. "Besides Geraldine herself."

"She's right," Geraldine said. "I never told you, but I used to run a thrift shop in Ochopee, FL after I left Vegas. Until Andrew blew everything away except Barney and me." Geraldine reached out and patted the old cash register. "We're both survivors. Only I've got a feeling Barney is gonna outlast me."

She could be right. I was ready to kill the old woman myself. "Well, I'm okay, too, in case you're interested," I grumbled. "Geraldine, how could you do this to me?"

Geraldine's brow furrowed. "Do *what*?"

"Are you kidding?" I hissed. "You stole all the money I had left to make something of this place. To make something of *myself*!"

Geraldine shook her head. "Hold on a minute. Take it easy, kid. It ain't what you think."

"It's *exactly* what I think!" I yelled. "You took the $2500 refund we got from the fair being cancelled and ran off and squandered it in Vegas!"

"Well, that's true," Geraldine said. "I did take the money, and I did run off to Vegas."

"Leaving me here to run the shop while you blew all the money I had!" My eyes brimmed with tears. "This is even worse than the time you blackmailed me into working for you. How could you do it?"

Geraldine held up a trembling hand. "I went to Vegas to see a specialist," she said. "I've got Parkinson's Disease."

"What?" I gasped.

"It's gotten too bad to hide it anymore," she said, hanging her head. "This trip to Vegas was my last hurrah. I won't be going again."

I blanched. "I ... I'm sorry you're sick, Geraldine. Truly I am. But your so-called 'last hurrah' was *mine*, too. I'm done for, and so is my dream of having my own business."

"I'm sorry, Val," Geraldine said. "But in this life, everything you do is a chance. There ain't no guarantees."

I shook my head, so angry I couldn't see straight. "I took a chance giving you the money to sponsor the fair. I was supposed to get that $2500 refund. But you took it for yourself, and now my future is black."

"I sure did take the money," Geraldine said. "And I won big."

I shook my head. "You call ruining me a *win*?"

"Lordy no!" Geraldine said, grabbing me by both arms. "I won *in Vegas*, Val! Enough to pay off everything you and I owe. Our future isn't black. It's *in* the black!"

I suddenly felt faint. "It is?"

"You're darn tootin' it is!" Geraldine's eyes gleamed with pride. She waved a Vanna White arm around at the destroyed front of the shop. "And don't forget, when I'm dead all of this is yours."

I glanced around at the broken windows and waterlogged merchandise. "Gee, how can I ever thank you enough?"

Geraldine laughed and smacked me on the back. "Cheer up, kid. Compared to Andrew, this ain't all that bad. Look around."

"Huh? At what?"

Geraldine pointed a shaky finger past my shoulder. I turned around to find that beyond the tangled melee of clothes and household debris flailed around in the front of the store, my shop, Simply Smashing, stood safely tucked away in the back, untouched by the storm.

"Holy smokes!" I screeched. "It's a miracle!"

Geraldine laughed. "Don't go ballistic on me."

I gasped. "Ballistics!" I whirled back around and grabbed the old woman by the shoulders. "Geraldine, all the evidence points to you as the one who killed Orville!"

The old woman's face puckered. "What are you talking about, *I'm* the killer?"

"Geraldine Jiggles!" a man's voice rang out.

I turned to see Sergeant McNulty striding rapidly toward us. "Come with me," he said to Geraldine. "You're wanted for questioning in the murder of Orville Ledbetter."

"But I'll miss my hair appointment at Curl Up & Dye!" Geraldine protested.

"You should've thought about that before you made an appointment for someone else to do that exact same thing." McNulty said, taking her by the arm.

"What exactly have you got on me?" Geraldine demanded.

"You want to go there?" McNulty asked. "Okay. The bullets we found in your Junior Commando came from the same box of shells we found in Ledbetter's gym bag."

Langsbury and I gasped.

"So what?" Geraldine said. "I found those bullets in the grass the day before the shootout. It would've been a crime to let them go to waste."

"The only crime *I* see at the moment is murder with intent," Mc-Nulty said. "You have the right to remain silent. I suggest you use it."

Langsbury and I stood, mouths ajar, as McNulty led Geraldine out the door and into his squad car. As he climbed into the driver's seat and got on his walkie-talkie, Winky's head popped up in the frame of the blown-out front window.

"Y'all decent?" he called out, then cautiously made his way into the shop carrying the broken letter D from our sign.

"Winky, what are you doing here?" I asked.

He grimaced and nodded in the direction of McNulty's squad car. "You ought to know, Val-Pal. Nothing draws a crowd faster'n cop cars at the neighbor's house."

Chapter Thirty-Five

"Lawdy mercy," Winky said as the three of us watched McNulty haul Geraldine out of Belated Rooms for questioning regarding the sudden demise of Orville Ledbetter.

"You can say that again," I said. "Geez. It's not looking good for her."

"Hey," Langsbury said, poking me with a boney finger. "My sister might be a skinflint and a hardnose, but she's no murderer."

"I hope not," I said. "But did you know Orville left everything to her in his will? And I heard her on the phone the other day talking to someone about trying to 'get rid of a total waste of time and money.'"

Langsbury's confident expression collapsed. "Dang. She's been dating Orville for half a year. All she did was complain about him being not worth the trouble."

"That don't sound too good," Winky said, grabbing a broom and sweeping up the glass shattered by the tornado.

I shook my head. "I don't get it. Even if Orville was a pain in the butt, why kill him?"

"The money," Langsbury said. "I write mystery novels. It's always about the money."

I frowned. "Your sister knows darn well the will would draw suspicion right to her. Geraldine's greedy, but she's not stupid."

"Maybe she didn't know about it," Langsbury said.

"Hold on," Winky said, stopping to pick up a soggy stuffed animal. "If Ms. G didn't do it, who did?"

I frowned. "Tom told me it had to be someone with access to Orville, because the bullet that killed him came from the same lot as the box of ammo found in his duffel bag."

"*Gym* bag," Winky corrected.

"How do you know the bullets came from his bag?" Langsbury asked.

"On account a I found his bag by the pool the mornin' of the shootout," Winky said. "I put it in the Lost & Found closet in the clubhouse for safe keepin'. We found half a box a .38 caliber bullets inside it when we done our stakeout yesterday."

"Two days later?" Langsbury said. "Anyone could've put the bullets in there after the shootout."

"I don't think so," I said. "That bag was nasty. I wouldn't have touched it with a ten-foot pole."

"Then why would *he*?" Langsbury asked, nodding at Winky.

"Because," I said. "He's a guy."

Winky smiled proudly. "Found his gun in the bag, too!"

Langsbury's brow furrowed. "Could he have—"

"Killed himself?" I said. "No, Tom said his gun was too corroded to fire. That means nobody could've killed Orville with it, including himself."

"Wait a second," Langsbury said. "Geraldine told McNulty she found the bullets in the grass. Is that even possible?"

"Yes!" I said. "The gym bag was ragged on the bottom. In fact, bullets fell out of it when we moved it out of the closet, right Winky?"

Winky grinned. "Sure is. And we all know Geraldine's a bona fide junkernecker."

"Junkernecker?" Langsbury asked.

"Scrapper," I said. "She'd pick up junk off the side of the road."

"Or anywhere else she could find it," Langsbury said, glancing around at the soggy array of secondhand stuff in the shop.

"Hey! You know what?" Winky said. "We sure did see a lot a thangs with bullet holes in 'em when we went junkerneckin' in her trailerhood."

"Yeah, but what's that—"

"Like that old toaster," Winky said. "You still got it?"

"I think so," I said. "Hang on." I walked over to my shop and collected the toaster. Like the microwave I'd murdered earlier, the toaster rattled as I carried it over to Winky. I shook it. A spent bullet fell out.

"Well, I'll be," Winky said. "Geraldine shot that thang up good."

Langsbury scoffed. "Why would she shoot up perfectly good junk, when she could sell it in her shop for cash?"

Suddenly, a thought hit me—not unlike a bullet between the eyes.

"Oh, my word!" I gasped. "I think I know what happened!"

Chapter Thirty-Six

I ran for the front door of Belated Rooms, intent on hightailing it to the police station to share my brilliant theory with Sergeant McNulty.

But one foot out the door and I was reminded that I wasn't in Kansas anymore. (Or maybe I was.) Tornado debris still littered Corey Avenue, making a quick getaway impossible.

Instead of running, I, Winky, and Angela Langsbury were forced to pick our way down the street to our cars parked outside the cordoned-off disaster zone.

"What's this brainstorm you've got?" Langsbury asked, hot on my heels. "Who do you think killed Orville?"

"Not *who*," I said. "*What*."

"Oh! I knew it!" Winky said. "It was that space alien, weren't it?"

"Argh!" I said, sprinting up to my car. "I'll explain it all once we get to the police station. Everybody follow me!"

• • • •

LIKE A CONGA LINE OF kooks in cars, Shabby Maggie and I led the charge down Central Avenue with Winky's blue van and Langsbury's faded silver Buick trailing in single file behind me. After hitting every red light along the way, I finally pulled into the police station on the corner of 1st Avenue N and 13th Street, parked my car and jumped out.

"Wait for us!" Winky hollered as I sprinted to the glass door of the shiny new SPPD headquarters.

"I'll meet you inside," I said. "Take care of Langsbury!"

"As in what are you talking about?" Langsbury said. "I can take care of myself. Now go help my sister!"

I nodded, then burst into the station. I ran up to the reception desk and startled the young receptionist with my gasping urgency. "I demand to see Officer McNulty now!" I said.

"Ma'am, please," the receptionist said. "Have a seat. I'll ring the Sergeant. Could I have your name?"

"Fremden. Tell him I'm here with proof of Geraldine's innocence."

"Oooh!" the receptionist said, her eyes sparkling with delight. "This is just like in the movies!"

Too nervous to sit, I paced in front of the desk until Winky and Langsbury made their way inside and joined me.

"What's going on?" Langsbury asked.

"Waiting for McNulty," I said.

"Um, Ms. Fremden?" the receptionist called out.

"Yes," I said, sprinting over to the desk.

"Um ... Sergeant McNulty is on his way," she said, pushing her glasses up on her nose. "And he said this had better be good."

Chapter Thirty-Seven

"**I**t was an accident!" I yelled as Sergeant McNulty entered the lobby of the SPDP. "It had to be a ricochet bullet!"

"What are you talking about Fremden?" McNulty said, glaring at me as he crossed the room with a tall, lanky man wearing a white lab coat.

"The bullet that killed Orville," I said. "That explains why nobody heard a thirteenth gunshot during the shootout. One of the .38 caliber bullets fired by either Geraldine or Rooster hit something, ricocheted off it, and accidently struck Orville between the eyes."

The man in the lab coat shot McNulty a glance. "That *would* help account for why the bullet was so mangled."

"Come on, Cleever," McNulty said to the man. "You're a ballistics expert. What are the odds of a stray bullet hitting an archery target then pinging backwards, traveling a hundred yards, passing through the holes in a chain-link fence, and striking someone right between the eyes?"

Cleever stroked his orange beard. "Well, it's not *impossible*, but it would require an astronomical stroke of bad luck."

"Well, sir," I said, puffing out my chest, "I happen to be an expert in astronomically bad luck."

"She ain't kiddin'," Winky said. "I can vouch for her."

"Were there any other obstacles in between the archery targets and the pool?" Cleever asked, taking off his glasses and rubbing his eyes.

"Yes," McNulty said. "I surveyed the area. Between the shootout and the clubhouse there were quite a few obstacles, including several oak trees and a metal dunking booth."

"And a pile a porta potties," Winky added.

"Right," McNulty said. He turned to Cleever. "Still think it's possible?"

He shook his head. "No. I just can't see it happening. At least, not from the archery station. Could there have been another point of origin for the bullet?"

An image of the shiny gold cartridges lying in the grass beside the pool popped into my mind. "What if someone fired a gun the exact same time as one of the 12 shots fired during the shootout?" I asked. "At close range. From where the bullets were found in the grass?"

"The timing would have to be perfect," Cleever said. "And that wouldn't account for the mangled state of the bullet, even if it grazed the chain-link fence on its trajectory."

"Geez," I said. "Then where else could the bullet have come from?"

"That's the 64-million-dollar question," McNulty said. "That's why we're focusing on motive, of which your friend Ms. Jiggles appears to have plenty."

"Sorry, lady," Cleever said to me. "It was a good thought, but we've already played out these angles. They just don't fit the evidence."

I frowned. "Well, thank you for listening. You, too, Sergeant McNulty." I turned to Winky and Langsbury. "Let's go."

* * * *

I WAS HALFWAY TO SHABBY Maggie when something Wynona said made my brain tingle with another idea. "Hold on!" I yelled to Winky and Langsbury. "I'm going back in!"

"What?" Winky hollered as I ran back into the SPDP. But I didn't have time to explain.

"Sergeant McNulty!" I yelled as I burst through the door and into lobby. "Wait!"

McNulty was still talking with Cleever. He looked over to me. "What now, Fremden?"

"What if someone hit a bullet?" I asked. "You know, with a hammer or something? Could that make it fire accidently?"

McNulty shook his head. "Do you even know how a bullet works, Fremden?"

Cleever shot McNulty a look. "Go on, Sarge. I'll take it from here."

"Thanks. Good luck," McNulty said, then unlocked a metal security door and disappeared behind it.

"Come with me," Cleever said. "All three of you. I don't want to have to explain this more than once."

"Yes, sir!" Winky said, saluting.

We followed Cleever through the same door McNulty used. He led us down a hall and into what looked like a classroom.

"Have a seat," he said, then drew a picture of a cartridge on a whiteboard. "Lots of people think a bullet is just a bullet," he said. "But that's just the tip of the iceberg."

Cleever pointed to the top of the cartridge, then chuckled at his own joke. "A cartridge is actually a complete assembly, made up of the outer casing, a primer agent, gunpowder, and the bullet. While the gunpowder provides the force needed, it's just the explosion. It's the *gun barrel* itself that provides the containment needed to actually propel the bullet in an outward trajectory."

"I don't understand," I said.

"What he's sayin' is, if'n you hit a bullet with a hammer, it might explode, but it wouldn't go nowheres," Winky said.

"Exactly," Cleever said.

I chewed my lip, desperately aware that my theory was going down the tubes. If it did, it would take Geraldine along with it. Suddenly, another idea hit me.

"What if you struck a bullet—I mean a *cartridge*—with a moving object," I asked. "Like a lawnmower blade."

"Highly unlikely it would ignite the gunpowder," Cleever said. "Even if it did, it would still merely explode like a weak firecracker."

My nose crinkled. "Really? It wouldn't be any stronger than that?"

"I'm afraid not." Cleever pointed at the cartridge he'd drawn on the whiteboard. "You see, without a gun's cylindrical barrel to focus the direction of the explosion, the gunpowder would blow out in all directions at the same time. It might propel the bullet a foot or two, but that's all. You'd be more likely to be injured by the blades slinging the whole cartridge out of the grass chute."

Winky nodded and rubbed his freckled chin. "Well, I'll be. Hey Mr. Science Man. What would happen if that there lawnmower blade hit a plain little ol' bullet that'd already been fired?"

"Yeah!" I said. "People get injured by rocks flying out of mowers. Why not an already spent bullet?"

Cleever, aka Mr. Science Man, blanched. He tilted his head, stroked his beard, then began to speak. "You know, while it's highly unlikely, if the mower blade hit the bullet in a way that propelled it with significant force and trajectory, I believe it's theoretically possible for it to cause injury or even death."

Winky poked me on the shoulder. "Was that a yes or a no?"

"A yes," I said, then turned to Cleever. "Right?"

Cleever nodded. "And that would nicely explain the mangled state of the bullet. But all this is moot unless there was an actual mower in the equation. Was there?"

"Yes!" I grinned. "When I left the pool to go to the shootout, Rooster was still mowing the grass in that area. Rooster's mower must've struck a spent bullet lying in the grass after Orville had gotten into the pool. That accounts for the timing *and* the lack of a random gunshot!"

Langsbury grinned. "Sounds like we have our answer, Mr. Science Guy. Now let's go save my sister!"

Chapter Thirty-Eight

"**A**nd that's how we believe it went down Sarge," Cleever said, wrapping up our new explanation of the ballistics evidence to McNulty, who'd joined us in the classroom.

"It's an interesting theory," McNulty said, glancing over at Cleever's whiteboard drawing of a gun cartridge. He turned to me. "Actually, it's just the kind of crazy idea I'd expect from you, Fremden. But it fits the evidence. How did you even think of it?"

I smiled. "I owe it all to Goober."

McNulty's brow furrowed. "Don't you mean Goggles?"

"No, sir. *Goober*. Him and Wynona Bologna."

"Argh!" McNulty groaned. "Enough with all those stupid nicknames! Explain what you mean before I lock you up for being a public nuisance!"

"The smell of death," I said. "Wynona did a crystal ball reading for me. She told me that 'the smell of death was everywhere' when Goggles died."

McNulty shook his head. "That's your proof? That a fortune teller told you *death stinks*?"

"No, sir. She said that 'the smell of death was everywhere.' That's where Goober comes in."

"Who the hel—" McNulty caught himself. "Who is Goober?"

"Only the smartest friend I ever had," Winky chimed in.

I shot him some side-eye. "Thanks, Winky."

McNulty glared at us. "I'm waiting."

"Goober was a good friend of ours, sir," I explained. "An intellectual, a weirdo, and a really nice guy. Anyway, I remember him once telling me that the aroma of fresh-cut grass was actually a chemical distress call. He said the plants gave it off to warn other nearby plants to start moving nutrients to their roots before they got cut down themselves."

"In other words, they were trying to save their neighbors while they themselves were dying," Langsbury said.

"Yes," I said. "And the day Rooster hit that spent bullet, he was mowing them down, and—"

"And the smell of death was everywhere," McNulty said.

I nodded. "Exactly. Somewhere along the way, Rooster's mower blade hit a spent bullet that had fallen out of Orville Ledbetter's tattered gym bag. And, unfortunately, that bullet found its mark between Orville's eyes."

"In other words, Ledbetter inadvertently caused his own death," McNulty said.

"Yes." I sighed. "You know, I don't get it. Orville had all the money in the world. Why would he carry a ragged old gym bag when he could easily afford a new one?"

"Why would he live in filth in a dirty old trailer, hoarding junk up to its rafters?" Langsbury asked.

"Greed?" McNulty asked.

"It don't really matter," Winky said. "He who dies with the most junk is still dead."

Chapter Thirty-Nine

I hung up the phone and shook my head, barely believing my own ears. Sergeant McNulty had just informed me that he was releasing Geraldine, and that I'd been instrumental in solving the Case of the Pistoled Pervert.

Actually, he'd called it the Ledbetter Case.

Po-*tay*-to, po-*tot*-o.

Apparently, you can't call someone a pervert in the newspaper, either. I just read an email from Saurwein that included a preview of the article she plans on running in this week's *Beach Gazette*.

In it, Saurwein credits me in helping solve Orville's death. She even favorably mentions my new shop, calling Simply Smashing "a smashing success." Maybe the crusty reporter has changed her caustic ways. Or maybe it didn't hurt that I let her have a free, 30-minute trial run at my shop (and threw in a pinata with her boss's face pinned onto it).

Epilogue

As you've probably figured out by now, we Floridians are tough old birds. A week has passed since that lousy tornado gave a twisted black eye to nearly every shop on Corey Avenue. But if you were to visit our little corner of the world now, you'd never think anything bad had ever happened here.

That includes Belated Rooms, though you might not recognize it.

For the past seven days, everybody I know and love has turned out to help clean up the mess, repair the damage, and make everything brand new. And I do mean *everything*.

"You about done fixing the sign?" I asked Winky as he lumbered into the shop with a drill in one hand, a roll of duct tape in the other.

"High-ho silver to the rescue!" he said, patting the roll of tape. "Come take a look."

I followed my freckled friend out into the heat and sunshine. I didn't know what I was expecting to see, but it wasn't *this*.

"I couldn't spell belated," Winky said, "on account a the 'D' bein' all busted up and whatnot. I couldn't find the missin' part, so I changed it into an 'L', and spelled out something I knew with the letters I had left."

"I can see that," I said, looking up at the sign. What used to be Belated Rooms was now Late BloomeRs.

"Not bad for reintarnation, eh?" Winky said.

"Reintarnation?"

"Yep." Winky beamed. "Brought back to life by a redneck."

I laughed. "Well, if anybody was ever a late bloomer, it's me."

A rusty red pickup truck screeched up to the shop. A skunk-haired old woman in a wild print top, stretch pants, and lime-green Crocs tumbled out.

"You do that, Winky?" Geraldine asked, jabbing a crooked finger up at the mismatched sign.

Winky glanced down at the asphalt, his ballcap in his hand. "Yes, ma'am."

"How much did it cost?" she demanded.

Winky looked up and shrugged. "Nothin' but sweat and duct tape, Ms. G."

"Then I love it," Geraldine said, then hobbled into Late BloomeRs.

I smirked at Winky. "Well, if Geraldine likes it, you've got my seal of approval, too. Thank you so much!"

I put my arm around him and we went inside the shop. Geraldine was busy making a call on the land line. I walked over and whispered, "You could've been more enthusiastic about the sign, you know."

Geraldine stopped dialing and shot me some side-eye. "Once you hit a certain age, kid, you become permanently unimpressed by darn near everything."

"Well, I'm impressed about your Vegas winnings. Thanks for paying me back the whole $4500. You didn't have to."

"Of course I did. We're partners. Now get outta my way. I need to make a call."

Geraldine dialed the phone. "Hello? I told you for the last time, I want to be rid of this waste of time and money! I'm not calling again, and I'm not paying you another dime!" She slammed the phone receiver down.

I blanched.

Oh my gosh! That's what she said last week. When I thought she was paying someone to get rid of Orville! Is she ...

"Um, Geraldine?" I said. "Who were you—"

"Can you believe this crap?" Geraldine rolled her eyes. "Who in their right mind wants to pay $69 a month for a landline anymore? I've been trying to cancel it for a month!"

The front door to the shop screeched open like a toad with strep throat. Apparently, not even a tornado could kill those rusty hinges.

"Hey there!" Davy Eber said, poking his head inside. "Looks like you've got the shop back in shipshape!"

"Thanks to Winky," I said.

Winky blushed. "T'weren't nothin. Hey, what kinda name is Eber?"

"Scottish," Davy said. "Why?"

Winky grinned. "I heard bein' Scottish could get a guy kilt."

I glanced over at the front window and spotted Winky's old blue van pulling up. "Looks like Winnie's here."

"I'll go get her!" Winky said, then rushed out the door. I was about to follow him when Eber grabbed my elbow.

"I need to talk to you," he whispered. "Geraldine's palsy is really slowing her down."

"It may have slowed me down, but it hasn't shut me up!" Geraldine said.

"No," Davy said. "I don't think *anything* could do that. What I mean is, you're going to need more help around here. Admit it."

"I can still pull my weight," Geraldine said. "You've got antique equipment too, but it still works."

My nose crinkled. "What?"

Davy put his arm around Geraldine. "We're in love."

"Oh," I stuttered. "Well, congratulations."

"Thanks, kid," Geraldine said. She smiled at Davy. "I feel lucky. But I also feel cursed."

"You mean with palsy?" I asked.

Geraldine shook her head. "No. With being too stubborn to ask for anyone's help."

"Oh." I winced. "Me, too."

"Stubbornness can be good if you channel it properly," Geraldine said. "I'll admit I can't do all the things I used to do. But if you're willing, I can teach you the ropes of running this business for profit, instead of losing money."

"Wait," I said. "I want to know something. What would you have done if you'd lost all my money in Vegas?"

Geraldine nodded like a wise sage. "In life, some things are better left unpondered."

I thought of Geraldine and Eber together in bed. "You know what? You're right."

• • • •

THE FRONT DOOR TO THE thrift shop squeaked open again. "Here comes the bride!" Winky called out.

A plump woman with red glasses and a black bob haircut came bustling in pushing a baby carriage.

"Oh!" I squealed. "Let me see him!"

Winky picked the baby boy up out of the carriage and held him in his arms for us all to see. He took his tiny hand and waved it. "Little Huey says howdy, y'all!"

"Howdy!" we all said back to the freckle-faced little cherub.

Once again, the door to Late BloomeRs creaked open. This time Tom came through the door. He held it open for J.D. and Laverne to pass through.

"Looks like you two have been golfing again," I said to the men. Clad in nearly identical plaid shorts and golf shirts, they looked like twins, except Tom was twice as tall as J.D.

"And *I've* been baking!" Laverne called out, grinning from ear to ear in her gold lame jumpsuit.

The long-legged ex-showgirl burst through the door holding a giant sheet cake. A collective gasp sounded in the room. (Laverne's cooking wasn't exactly lethal, but if you ate it, you might wish you were dead.)

"I couldn't stop her," J.D. whispered as he walked up to me carrying a golf club.

"What was your plan?" I whispered back. "To knock her out with that club?"

"No!" he grimaced. "Just a simple little 'trip and fall.' Of the *cake*, of course."

"It's chocolate with secret sprinkles!" Laverne gushed, setting the cake on the plexiglass counter.

"Wait!" I cried out, but it was too late.

The counter, cracked during the storm, collapsed under the weight of Laverne's cake. It tumbled down through the broken plexiglass and landed—icing down—on the linoleum floor.

"Oh, no!" Laverne cried out. "But I made the icing special with my last can of Krassco I found on Craigslist!"

Tom leaned in and whispered in my ear, "Somewhere out there an angel just earned its wings."

"It's okay!" Winnie said, running over to comfort Laverne. "I brought donuts!" She reached under the baby carriage and pulled out a boxful. "Help yourself. There's plenty more in the van!"

J.D. sighed with relief and took a chocolate glazed donut. He admired it like a philosopher. "That man is richest whose pleasures are cheapest. Thoreau."

Winky grinned, his mouth full of cake donut. "Well, I don't know about that, but I'm *thorough*ly enjoyin' this donut!"

. . . .

WE'D POLISHED OFF THE first box of donuts and Winky was heading out to the van for reinforcements. But when he opened the door to the shop, a horde of people came rushing in.

I'd been expecting Milly, her husband Vance, and Angela Langsbury. But I was surprised to see Wynona and Finkerman also in the mix.

"Looks good in here," Langsbury said. "But I still expect to see you in class tomorrow."

"You got it, teach," I said.

"Yeah, nice redo of the digs," Finkerman said. "I guess even a mushroom cloud has a silver lining."

"Gee, thanks," I said.

Finkerman smirked. "I have to say, you're really rocking those mom jeans."

I laughed. "You know what you'd look good in? A *coffin*."

"Ouch." Finkerman laughed and handed me a business card. "Actually, that's the perfect segue. I now do estate planning—as well as my other fine services."

I laughed. "How about you and your fine services go eat a donut."

The pasty-faced attorney smoothed his frizzy red combover and grinned. "I thought you'd never ask."

Wynona smiled at me and walked over. "Don't let him bother you," she said, winking an eyelid covered in purple sparkly eyeshadow. "Once you start to love yourself, it doesn't matter who else doesn't love you."

I grinned. "You're right about that. But wrong about me and Finkerman. We love each other, just not like most people do."

"Hey everybody!" Milly called out.

I glanced over to see my best friend already decked out in overalls, boots, a helmet and protective eyewear.

"Yikes," I said to Vance. "I may have made a monster out of her."

He grinned. "How can I ever thank you?"

"Welcome to Late Bloomers!" Milly squealed, raising her hammer high. "Who's ready for their therapy session?"

"Milly!" I said. "You finally got the name right!"

She winked. "And so did *you*. Late Bloomers is so much better than Begruntled Rooms."

"Hey Val, can I use my golf club?" J.D. asked.

"To smash stuff? Sure." I gave him a thumbs up. "Why not? But wait until you get inside my part of the shop or you'll have hell to pay with Geraldine.

J.D. eyed a lamp that looked as if it could've been fashioned from elephant dung. "Hmm," he said. "Smashing that thing just might be worth it."

"Come on, everybody!" Milly said, leading the charge. "That junk isn't going to smash itself!"

As I watched everyone make a beeline for my little enterprise, Simply Smashing, I felt a familiar pair of arms wrap around me.

"Looks like you've got a hit on your hands," Tom said.

I laughed. "Was that pun intentional or not?"

Tom grinned. "I plead the fifth."

I kissed Tom, then settled back into his arms. The tornado had done its damage. But looking around at the shop now, I realized it had swept the place clean of everything that no longer held any value.

It wasn't exactly the fresh start I'd always imagined. It was so much more than that.

As my new-found family celebrated our rebirth with laughter and hammers and donuts and golf clubs, I was certain I could hear Glad's voice amidst the merriment;

"Good on you, Kiddo. Sometimes in the winds of change, you find your new direction."

THE END

Thanks so much for reading *The Devil Wears Stretch Pants!* It's book four in the *A Val Fremden Humorous Mystery Series.*

If you're new to Val Fremden, you might want to check out her first series, Val Fremden Midlife Mysteries. The nine-book series is available on Amazon here:

https://www.amazon.com/dp/B07FK88WQ3

While you're there, I'd be grateful if you took a minute to leave a review for *this* book. I appreciate every single one! Here's a handy link:

https://www.amazon.com/dp/B0DS8ZGR9T

• • • •

WANT TO STAY IN TOUCH and get a laugh in your Facebook feed every day? Join my Facebook page at:

* Facebook: https://www.facebook.com/valandpalspage/

Want to reach me by email? Or join my newsletter and be the first to hear about new releases and deals? Here's how:

* Newsletter Link: https://dl.bookfunnel.com/fuw7rbfx21

* Website: https://www.margaretlashley.com

* Email: contact@margaretlashley.com

Thanks again. I appreciate you!

All my best,

Margaret

About the Author

W hy do I love underdogs?

Well, it takes one to know one. Like the main characters in my novels, I haven't led a life of wealth or luxury. In fact, as it stands now, I'm set to inherit a half-eaten jar of Cheez Whiz...if my siblings don't beat me to it.

During my illustrious career, I've been a roller-skating waitress, an actuarial assistant, an advertising copywriter, a real estate agent, a house flipper, an organic farmer, and a traveling vagabond/truth seeker. But no matter where I've gone or what I've done, I've always felt like a weirdo.

I've learned a heck of a lot in my life. But getting to know myself has been my greatest journey. Today, I know I'm smart. I'm direct. I'm jaded. I'm hopeful. I'm funny. I'm fierce. I'm a pushover. And I have a laugh that lures strangers over, wanting to join in the fun.

In other words, I'm a jumble of opposing talents and flaws and emotions. And it's all good.

I enjoy underdogs because we've got spunk. And hope. And secrets that drive us to be different from the rest.

So, dare to be different. It's the only way to be!

All my best,

Margaret

www.ingramcontent.com/pod-product-compliance
Lightning Source LLC
Chambersburg PA
CBHW022157240626
47153CB00007B/2711